WAR HEROES

WORLD WAR II ADVENTURES IN FRANCE AND BELGIUM

DANIEL WRINN

This book is a work of fiction. Any references to historical events, real people, or real places are used fictitiously. Other names, characters, places and events are products of the author's imagination, and any resemblances to actual events or places or persons, living or dead, is entirely coincidental.

CONTENTS

Chapter 1	1
Chapter 2	9
Chapter 3	17
Chapter 4	23
Chapter 5	31
Chapter 6	39
Chapter 7	45
Chapter 8	53
Chapter 9	61
Chapter 10	69
Chapter 11	79
Chapter 12	87
Chapter 13	95
Chapter 14	103
Chapter 15	111
Chapter 16	121
Chapter 17	129
Chapter 18	137
Book 2 in the John Archer Series:	145
Also By Daniel Wrinn	147
About the Author	151

1

May 10th, 1940

Our small Renault car zipped along the dusty French road like a little brown bug fleeing for its life. The ride out of Paris was depressing and thrilling at the same time. My skin trembled with goosebumps as we skirted past the long lines of army cars and marching troops.

Lieutenant Dubois' military papers cleared the way through every barrier thrown up across the road. These papers were like a magic charm. Not only were they signed by the highest military authorities, but by the president of France himself. I guess my father really had connections here.

I sat in the car with my arms crossed and my jaw clenched tight. Why did I have to leave Paris? Why was I running away? What real danger? I was having a ton of fun in Paris. Why am I running away? Because danger *might* come to Paris? There *might* be a war soon? I guess I was only following my father's instructions, but still, the thought of leaving Paris so soon twisted and stabbed my stomach.

Lieutenant Dubois gripped the steering wheel. The light from the Frenchman's eyes had drained. No more jokes, no more funny anecdotes about Paris. Now he was grim and looking scared. He clutched the wheel tight. Every so often, he tilted his head out the window to look into the sun-filled blue sky, blinking with anxious fear. I followed his look, but I saw nothing.

"I still don't understand," I said. "England? Why do I have to go to England?"

"Your father wants you to go to England for your safety." Dubois leaned closer into the steering wheel. "'Why?' I don't know. I received a wireless message. In it, your father said you were to leave for London at once. I'm going to take you to Calais, where you'll board a destroyer. That's all I know."

"So, my fun in Paris is over because of the German invasion of Belgium?"

"*Oui*, yes," Lieutenant Dubois said, clearly trying to keep his voice polite.

Ugh. So much for my French vacation. And what about Audrey? In my three weeks living on the *Avenue des Champs-Élysées*, I'd already fallen in love with a golden-haired Swedish girl. I didn't even have a chance to say goodbye before I was scooped up like a baguette and carried away—for my own safety.

I'm an American. This war doesn't involve my country. We're neutral, and I hope we stay that way. I would've thought everyone had learned their lesson from the Great War. I'm not getting involved in any European war. I want my freedom. I want to live and love. I want to be a pilot and see the world.

I don't understand why my father has to meddle in my life. Paris is safe. Nothing will ever happen to me in Paris. What does he think: the Nazi's will conquer France? Occupy Paris? Nonsense. Always worrying and always ruining my fun. Just because he's some bigshot ambassador doesn't mean he can order me around, like I'm one of his staff. After I get to England, I'm going straight to the embassy and finding him. I'll give him a piece of my mind before we straighten this whole mess out. *Ooh Audrey*, I'll be back to see you soon . . .

Lieutenant Dubois dabbed at the wet beads of sweat from his face with his handkerchief. I realized how tired and weary he looked now. His eyes were drawn and haggard. His funny little mustache seemed to even droop from his fatigue. But despite his crisp uniform and the two rows of shiny metals, Lieutenant Dubois looked like he hadn't slept for days.

"What's the matter?" I asked. "You look worried. You think something's going to happen?"

Lieutenant Dubois shrugged. And for the five hundredth time, he peered up into the sky.

"Nothing's gonna happen. It's my neck, *mon Dieu!* It's a little stiff. Feels better when I move my head." Dubois tried to add a little laugh to pepper his words, but I knew he was full of it.

"Tell me the truth," I said. "You're looking for German airplanes, aren't you? You look worried. I saw you talking with a major before we left. Did you get any news?"

"We're holding back the Germans," Dubois said through clenched teeth. "Our troops, along with the English, are pouring into Belgium by the thousands. We'll throw *les Boches* back. They'll learn a lesson this time that they won't—"

Our car spun around a bend. In front of us was a road clogged with men, women, and children. A sea of people, horses, cows, goats, and even dogs swept toward us. Dubois slowed down as we approached wagons, carts, and even baby carriages piled high with household goods. Above it all rose a babble of frightened speech.

I pointed at the unfolding scene. "What is going on?"

Dubois didn't say a word. He slowed the car and stopped. Then opened the door and hopped onto the road. He slid his hand toward his holstered pistol as swarms of desperate humans advanced toward us. Lieutenant Dubois flung up his hand.

"Stop," he shouted in French. "What is the meaning of this?"

A thousand people answered his question in the same voice. "The Germans. Les Boches. They're coming," they screamed almost in unison. "They have broken through. They've taken everything. They are everywhere. They will slaughter us like cattle if they catch us. How far to Paris? Feels like we've walked for years. We're so tired. *Help us, help us*, please."

"Enough. Stop it," Dubois shouted. "The Germans will not break through. France's soldiers will fight her and defeat her again. Go back to your homes. You are a bunch of frightened fools—all of you. I'm ordering you. Go back to your homes, and you'll be safe. The Germans will not harm you."

An old woman clutching a bundle of clothing rushed up to Dubois. She shook her wrinkled fist in his face and screamed at the top of her voice. "Our soldiers? Where are they? I've seen them retreating. There are too many Germans. *Les Boches* have airplanes, tanks, and guns. I watch them shoot down everyone and anyone. I ask you again, where? Where's our army? Where's the English, where are they?" Tears slid down the old woman's cheek as her mouth continued to babble. "I will tell you. The Germans have killed them, killed them all."

"Be quiet, old woman," Lieutenant Dubois roared. "Enough of this kind of talk. Only spies could have filled you with these lies. This is what they want. To scare you, frighten you, and make you leave your homes to clutter up the roads. Listen to me—"

Lieutenant Dubois raised his voice louder, but it was less than a faint cry in the wilderness. Long lines of terror-stricken refugees drowned him out. It was like an enormous wave that parted in the middle as they swept by on both sides of our car. Dubois' face was beet red with fury. He ranted, he shouted, and he raved to no avail. His voice and his actions were only a waste of breath and energy. I tried to help him. I tried to reason with this massive, terrified humanity that swept by us in waves. I begged. I pleaded. I threatened. But it was as useless as ordering the sun to turn off its shine. No one paid any attention. I doubt if anyone even heard me. I got so tired of yelling and pleading and begging that I sat back in the car. My voice was exhausted, and my throat felt raw.

I looked at Lieutenant Dubois. He was a picture of misery, and I watched the anger well up in his cheeks. Tears rolled from his eyes while he worked his mouth, but no sound came out of his lips. He eventually got back into the car and sank behind the wheel.

"I'm so ashamed of my countrymen," Dubois said, staring ahead at the road. "This is the curse of war. People flee like chickens when war comes. They don't stop to think the reason. They think of nothing but their own lives. They behave like children."

I didn't know what to say. We sat in silence for a few moments. Then I reached over and squeezed his arm. In a soothing tone, I said, "It's okay, forget about it. Look, we'll be stuck here forever if we don't do something. Let's try to get off the side of the road. I can get out and push them to the side, and you can keep the car in a low gear, okay?"

Some anger had faded from Dubois' eyes. The corner of his mouth tilted into a faint smile, and he nodded his head. "On your orders, *mon Capitaine.* Yes, you get out and warn them away, and I'll drive the car off to the side of the road to pass them."

I nodded back to him and slid out of the car. As my feet touched the road, I felt my body caught in a torrent like a raging river. As if I was a chip of wood that was picked up and swept along. Several seconds passed before I regained my footing and forced my way back around to the front of the car. I put out both my hands and started waving as a steady stream of babbling refugees surrounded me on all sides.

It was a heartbreaking and tedious effort. Over a hundred

times, I came close to falling flat on the road under the Renault's slow-rolling wheels. But I pushed and shoved people to the side as the car inched forward. Over half an hour passed before our car made fifty yards. I was drenched in sweat, my hat was gone, and my clothes were being slowly torn. I looked back, and saw Dubois waving his arms, pointing and shouting. I shoved my way back toward him.

"It's useless. This is madness. We will get nowhere like this. The town of Beaumont is only a few kilometers ahead. There's an army post there. I'll request a new car and driver. I'm so embarrassed that this should happen."

More ragged refugees slammed into Lieutenant Dubois. Literally, a river of people. Dubois struggled and fought but was swept along. Seconds after, I was caught up by the moving masses. I had to either move with the stream of people or get trampled by the heavy wheel of an ox-cart or wagon. It wasn't possible to move, and it would have been suicide to push my way or fight through that packed throng of desperate people.

I took the only course open to me. I moved along with the river of refugees. Inch by inch, I worked my way to the edge of the stream and into a clear place. I waited to breathe and strain my eyes for a glimpse of Lieutenant Dubois, but the Frenchman was nowhere to be seen. He had been swallowed up by the torrent of desperate humanity, moving blindly forward. I thought about the troops in the long lines of army cars that we passed since leaving Paris. What would happen when these refugees ran into the Army? Who would give way, or would anybody? I thought about other French officers like Dubois trying to force their way through. Trying to force the refugees to abandon their furious flight and return home. It wasn't a pretty picture to imagine. An awful situation to even dare contemplate. Troops, tanks, and guns moving forward to meet the enemy but instead meeting thousands of their own countrymen.

What's wrong with these people? My heart raced,

pounding against my rib cage. As I breathed softly to myself and gulped, a new sound came to my ears. An entirely different sound. I could only think of tons of brick sliding down a slanting tin roof. Then I knew what it was. In that same instant, the rising hysterical screams started.

"Take cover! The Germans, *les Boches, les Allemands*!"

It was as if thousands of stampeding cattle broke ranks and scattered wildly in all directions. Carts and wagons were abandoned. Ditched where they'd come to a halt with their horses and oxen. I stayed where I was. I didn't move an inch. My body was frozen. I looked up at the cluster of dots trickling down from the blue sky. I blinked. The dots turned into planes. German planes. Messerschmitt 110s and Stuka dive bombers. They zoomed in at a furious pace. Winged messengers of doom howled down upon the road, choked with countless numbers of desperate refugees.

The lead planes opened fire. A jutting red flame spat downward. A savage chatter of aerial machine guns echoed above the blood-chilling thunder of the engines. I tore my eyes from the horrible sight. I glanced back to the road. It was filled with screaming men, women, and children directly underneath where the diving planes' bullets were cutting down humans like a scythe cuts wheat.

My feet were rooted to the ground. I stared in horror. One of the Stukas released a deadly bomb. The bomb struck the ground less than twenty feet from the edge of the road. Red, orange, and yellow flames erupted into the air. A billowing cloud of smoke filled with dirt, dust, and stones mushroomed upward. Then a mighty roar like the sounds of colliding worlds hammered straight into my face. The next thing I remember, I was flat on my back. I was panting and gasping for air while screams came from wounded refugees dying in every direction.

I saw an old woman, bowed down by bundles, feebly trying to get off the road and out from under the roaring armada of diving death. She took a few steps and then stumbled onto her knees. With one withered hand, she stretched out in an appeal for help, but no one came.

I sprang into action. I jumped to my feet.

That old woman, poor old woman. She was only one out of thousands trapped here dying. But I will never forget her sad plight and how instinctive her movements were. I leaped forward and dashed to her side. With one hand, I grabbed both of her bundles and put them under my arm.

"I'll help you," I said in my barely passable French. "Just lean on me. I'll get you to a safe place, don't worry."

The old woman's eyes showed me deep gratitude through her lined and tired face. "*Merci, Monsieur, merci*," she whispered into my ear and leaned on my arm.

I heard the eerie sound above the general din of people screaming, but I didn't see the dropping bomb. I didn't even take the time to glance upward. I grabbed the old woman by the waist and hauled her to the protection of a standing wagon. I pushed her down and spread my body over so that at least I could partially protect her from what I knew was coming.

I guess this is it. Only two months from my eighteenth birthday.

And then it came. A terrific crash of sound that seemed to split the earth wide open at the seams. Every bone in my body turned to jelly. The entire universe was one huge ocean of flashing light and fire. The ground rocked and trembled under my feet. Hands grabbed hold of me and lifted me to hover in a cloud of licking tongues of colored flames. All became dark as night and silent as a tomb, and then I knew no more.

2

WHEN I OPENED MY EYES, it was night. I was lying on my back under some trees. I stared up through bomb-shattered branches. A canopy of twinkling and glittering stars high above. For several seconds I waited there entirely still—not moving a muscle. What happened? Where am I? Why am I out here, under some trees in the dark?

Questions swirled through my brain. Then, as if someone had pulled a curtain aside, my memory came back slowly. It was a Stuka dive bomber. It had dropped its bomb close. I remember trying to shelter that old woman. We were on the road by a car, and I was under some trees. Why? Had the bomb blown me under the trees? I looked around again. Am I wounded or dazed? I don't feel any pain? Ugh, it's night. I must've been here for hours.

I pushed myself up to a sitting position and regretted the idea. It felt like a hundred sledgehammers banging inside my head. The night stars swirled around me. I closed my eyes and clenched my teeth until everything stopped spinning. The pounding in my head switched to a throbbing ache that I could barely stand without flinching.

For the next few moments, I sat on the grass, grabbing

different parts of my body, searching for broken bones or any wounds. Nothing was broken. The only injury was a goose egg on the left side of my head. I slowly pushed myself up and braced a hand against the tree trunk. I looked around in the darkness. My eyes had not adjusted, and my head still spun.

I was in a field, as far as I could tell, and there wasn't a road anywhere near. The stream of refugees, wagons, and carts on the road was gone. Like I was dropped into the very middle of nowhere. Puzzled by the strangeness of my newfound surroundings, I found the North Star and walked. Way off in the distance was a faint rumbling, like thunder far away, but I knew at once it was the roar of heavy guns. If I needed any more proof, I just had to look northeast. A faint glow of flames on the horizon made a line between the night sky and the earth.

"Where am I?" I shouted. I should have been blown to pieces. I don't even have a sprained ankle. Where is Lieutenant Dubois? All those poor refugees. I hope the French planes cut those Germans and gave them what—

In the distance to the left was a pair of moving lights. I started running. Must be some kind of car on a road. Maybe I could get a ride back to Paris. I'd be crazy to try to make it to Calais now. The best thing I could do is get back to Paris as fast as possible and ask for help.

I raced at top speed toward that pair of moving dim lights. Every step I took, a gnawing fear grew that I wouldn't make it in time. I reached the edge of the road less than twenty yards in front of those lights and paused. I ignored the danger of being run over in the dark and jumped to the middle of the road. I did jumping jacks, waving both of my arms, shouting at the top of my voice like a madman. The brakes squealed, and the car came to a jerking halt.

"What in the bloody hell are you doing?" a voice shouted from behind the lights. "I came close to running you down."

An English voice. Relief washed over me. I trotted toward

the lights and then around them to the driver's side. The car was an ambulance. A nice brand new one with the Red Cross painted above the words: British Volunteer Ambulance Service.

"Speak English?" the driver asked.

I looked at him. He wasn't in uniform. He wore civilian clothes and looked close to my age. Maybe even a few months younger. In the faint glow of the dashboard light, his face held a sarcastic expression. His hair fell down over his forehead an inch from his glowing blue eyes. I instantly liked him.

"You bet I speak English," I said and reached my hand out to shake. "I'm an American. My name is John Archer. But everyone calls me Archer."

"Mine's Barney James," the Englishman said. "Good to meet you, America, but why are you here? Look at you, did a bomb fall on you?"

I couldn't stifle a chuckle. "Sure came close. I just noticed your lights a few minutes ago. I'm trying to get back to Paris. How far away am I?"

"Paris?" Barney said. "It's over one hundred miles back. We're in Belgium, mate. Don't you know that? What happened anyway? You said you were bombed."

I was stunned for a handful of seconds and couldn't speak. Wait, this is Belgium? How? He must be wrong. I was sure Dubois and I hadn't been any further than seventy miles from Paris when we crashed into those refugees. Belgium? Did that bomb blow me thirty miles away? This is just crazy.

"Hop in and ride with me," Barney said. "I can't take you to Paris, but Courtrai is up ahead. Might be someone there who can take you back to Paris."

I nodded and hopped in. The gears shifted and the ambulance lurched forward. I told Barney about my experiences since getting on the road from Paris that morning. My new English friend didn't interrupt, but now and then, he took his eyes off the road and looked at me with a genuine smile.

"That was decent of you to help that old woman," Barney said when I'd finished. "We'd heard Germans were shooting and bombing refugees. A nasty business, but that's how Hitler wages war."

"Those poor people didn't have a chance," I said. "They were helpless. I don't see how Hitler thinks he can win the war that way."

Barney gripped the steering wheel of the ambulance. His knuckles were white. He looked over at me with flared nostrils and a high chin. "Hitler won't win this war. He might have us on the ropes for a bit, but in the end, we'll win just like before."

My neck and jaw stiffened. "I think part of his plan is to scare people onto the roads and clog up traffic so the troops can't get through."

"I saw that sort of thing today," Barney said. "I couldn't make more than five miles in six hours. I had to fight them off from stealing my ambulance and using it for a bus."

I glanced at my new English friend. His cheeks were pale from fatigue and he had a glassy stare. I reached out to touch the wheel. "You look exhausted. I had a pretty good sleep. I can take the wheel for a while? Just tell me which way to go."

Barney turned his head and frowned. "Not tired at all, mate. And no one drives this ambulance but me. Besides not much farther to go, only a few more miles."

"If you change your mind, let me know," I said. "You been driving an ambulance long? You go out and help pick up the wounded? Must've seen a lot of battles?"

"What's with all the questions?"

"Just making conversation, not trying to—"

"Strange thing," Barney said.

"Huh?"

"I said it's strange that I found an American in the middle of the road, when I did. You don't speak German, do you?"

I pressed my lips together into a tight line. "Are you asking me if I'm a German spy."

"Not directly. I said it's strange that—"

"Do I look like a spy to you?" I shouted. "I don't want any part of this stupid war. I'm here trying to spend the summer in Paris and now I'm in the middle of this mess."

Barney chuckled. He clearly enjoyed triggering this reaction from me. "Calm down, mate. I'm not accusing you of anything. Just stating a fact."

We spent the next few minutes in an awkward silence.

"I'm not really an ambulance driver," Barney said in a soft voice. "You have to be eighteen to join the volunteer service, and I'm still a couple months away. I was going to school outside Paris and my family decided I should come home to England."

"That sounds familiar," I said.

"Yesterday, several of these ambulances arrived at the Paris headquarters," Barney continued after a heavy sigh. "They'd been shipped to Paris as a mistake. They were needed in Belgium, and there weren't any regular volunteer drivers in Paris. Or not enough, anyway. I thought it would be fun to drive one before crossing the Channel home. We left Paris last night at midnight, and all lost track of each other. It's been fun, though I'll be glad when this trip ends."

"You've been driving since midnight?" I asked. "You can sure take it, Barney."

"Take it?" Barney's shoulders hunched, and he looked at me with a puzzled frown. "I don't know what you mean."

I laughed. "That's American slang for you. It means you got a lot of courage. That you're an okay guy."

"Thanks, Archer. But it doesn't take courage. I'm glad to do my bit to help the troops. We gotta beat these Germans. You know what I mean?"

"Ah, actually, no," I said. "This isn't my fight. I'd rather not get involved. I've got plans for my future that don't involve getting killed before my eighteenth birthday."

Barney wrinkled his nose and rubbed at his mouth.

For the next few miles, we lapsed into another silence. I stared at the dim red glow of burning buildings in the distance. So this is what war looks like. Apparently, it's begun in earnest. But what could I do? Even if I wanted to help, I'm an American, and America is neutral in this war.

My blood boiled today after what I saw. I didn't know much about Hitler and the Nazi's before today. Something inside of me yearned to help the French and British. Plenty of boys my age took part in the last war. But so many were hurt —hurt bad too. They lost arms and legs, so many dead. My father fought and was wounded. Two uncles died fighting in France. I swore I'd never get involved. But it would be fun to fight, to help defeat the Nazis. But what if I get hurt? Or killed? I'd never see Audrey again, or Paris. Nah, I'm not getting involved. Maybe I could offer my services as a pilot. I've almost got my license. I've already had a couple solo flights. I'm strong and big for my age. I could lie my way in. I'll talk to Father about it when I get to—

The ambulance came to a squealing halt.

"What's the matter?" I asked.

"I think I might have gotten us into a bit of a mess. We're lost. Actually, I don't have the foggiest clue where we are. I'm sorry, mate."

My skin tingled, and a jittery feeling rolled in my stomach. "I thought you said we were close to Courtrai?"

Barney shrugged his shoulders and sank down in his seat.

The night was quiet with no moon. Pitch dark out and hard to see anything. After several minutes, a faint rumbling got closer. Barney pointed at the dim approaching light.

"Here comes a car. Wait, sounds like a truck. What a racket."

Headlights shone along the road that led to the right.

They were bouncing up and down on the uneven surface. A banging noise in the engine made me think of a piece of farm equipment that threshes grain. I stepped into the glow of our ambulance's lights and waved my arms. The car or truck, or whatever it was, came to a stop with its gears clashing and grinding.

"Well Archer, looks like we're about to find out what it is." Barney said and walked toward the twin beams of light slowly approaching.

I followed behind my English companion, we'd only walked a few yards when we heard a harsh voice shout, "Halt!"

I froze. My eyes temporarily blinded as I blinked into the light. Barney caught his breath in a sharp gasp. My own heart pounded like a ping pong ball against my rib cage. A dryness stifled the back of my throat. Hobnailed boots clacked on the road. A figure of a soldier came into the light. He wore a bucket-shaped helmet. In his hands was a wicked-looking machine gun. He cautiously moved toward me. I saw his uniform clearly. My heart turned to ice, my hands felt clammy, cold, and damp.

It was a German soldier.

3

"GERMANS," Barney whispered out of the side of his mouth.

I stood stunned in a trance. I blinked. My throat swallowed hard while I tried to control the pounding of my heart.

The German soldier pulled up less than ten feet away. He stared at us. Another clacking of hobnailed boots and behind him a second figure walked out into the light. The second man was a German infantry officer. He kept one hand on his holstered Luger pistol and walked toward us.

"Hey there, mate," Barney said. "We're lost here. Where are we?"

"You're English?" the German officer asked in a heavy nasal voice. "Why are you here? An ambulance? Are you trying to sneak back through our lines? Keep your hands up, both of you." The German soldier patted us down for weapons.

"We're not armed, Captain," I said. "We're not soldiers. We're lost."

The German officer's face turned red. "I'm not a captain, I'm a lieutenant. You will address me as such. So you're not soldiers, then why do you have this ambulance? Why are you here?"

"I've already told you," Barney said in a calm voice. "We're lost. Now tell us the way to Courtrai and we'll be on our way."

"So you are an Englishman." The German officer took a step closer and cocked his head.

"And proud of it," Barney said and stiffened his back. "And this bloke here, if you must know, is an American mate of mine. Now, which way to Courtrai?"

The German officer said nothing for seconds that seemed like minutes. His lips pressed tight into a grimace on his sharp-featured face. Maybe he was disappointed he hadn't found a pistol or automatic rifle on either of us. He took a step back and stood with his fists bunched on his hips.

"An American and an Englishman," the German officer muttered. "This is unusual, even strange. And you say you don't know where you are?"

"That's right Lieutenant," I said. My muscles quivered, and heat flushed through my body. "Where are we anyway? What are you doing here? Are we in Germany?"

The lieutenant smiled, revealing a row of yellow-stained teeth. "I think you lie to me." He walked around us in a semi-circle. "Yes, I'm sure of that. I'll take you to the *Kommandant*. He'll get you to talk. Our enemies send boys like you to spy on us. The grown men must be too afraid. Can't fool me with your tricks."

I said, "Tricks? This is no trick. I told you the truth. We were on our way—"

"Don't even waste your breath," Barney said, putting his hand on my shoulder. "After he tells this story to his commanding officer, they'll let us go."

"So?" The German officer gave me a piercing look. "We will then see if you are spies, and if you are, it will go hard for you. Now! Get into that car in front of me."

The German lieutenant turned his head and snapped something at the soldier standing behind him. The soldier sprang into action. He jogged past us and climbed into the front seat of the ambulance.

I grabbed Barney's arm. "Don't worry. They can't do anything to us. Don't let them see we're worried."

"What did you say? What are you saying to him?" The lieutenant drew his Luger pistol.

I froze. My skin became clammy and I started to shake. I was determined to keep looking the German officer straight in the eye.

"I told him that the American consul would fix things up for us."

The German officer snorted. "Maybe," he said in a low growling voice. "We will see."

We walked to the car with our heads held up, shoulders back, and my chest jutted out. As we passed beyond the headlights, we plunged into darkness. For a moment, I saw nothing. Then my eyes got used to the change, and I saw it was a combination car and truck. Actually, it was an armored troop transport. Steel sheets protected the driver's seat, and instead of heavy-duty tires on the rear wheels, they were tractor treads. This truck could travel cross-country through mud and paved road.

The back of the truck held fifteen German soldiers, all armed with small machine guns. They looked down at Barney and me as the officer motioned them to make us to get into the transport—none of them spoke to us. Either they didn't understand English or were too afraid of the officer to speak. Barney and I climbed aboard in silence. We sat on a hard plank that served as seats. The officer got in beside the driver and growled an order.

The engine roared, the gears clanked and crashed, and the transport lunged forward. It was only off a few yards before it swung off the road and into the direction from where it had come. The direction was east, and as soon as I realized, I pressed my knee against Barney's. He returned the pressure. I hoped my new English friend understood the predicament we were in and wasn't planning anything stupid.

I gazed over the driver's shoulder and watched the road. Bombs and shells had torn the pavement up. The driver swerved to avoid wrecked ammunition wagons and artillery pieces strewn along the road. Big guns were smashed beyond recognition, surrounded by dead Belgian soldiers and refugees unable to escape the advancing German hordes.

A roar of airplane engines snatched my attention, and I gazed toward the sky. I couldn't see the planes. They were too high, but the pulsating beat of their engines told me they were Hitler's night bombers out on patrol. I clenched my fists. The thought crossed my mind of joining this fight. What if I was up there in a swift deadly pursuit or fighter plane. I've taken flying lessons for a few years. I could do it. My instructor said I was too reckless, but also that I was a natural flyer. What if I got shot down? What if I had to land a plane with a shot-up engine? What if I crashed into the ground and was ripped apart in a ball of fire? It would be much easier to avoid all this mess. It's not even my war, or my problem. Dizziness washed over me, my stomach hardened, my knees felt weak.

I turned to Barney. "I'd like to be up there in a Curtis P-Forty. I bet I could do something, or at least I could try to help."

Barney leaned in closer. "Are you a pilot, Archer?"

"I've flown solo. Someday I hope to get my private pilot's license, but I'm still too young. Flying is the best thing. There's nothing like it. Can you hear those planes up there?"

"German Heinkel bombers, I think," Barney said. "Or maybe Dorniers, I can't tell by the sounds. I'm crazy about flying too. I joined an aero club back home. I got a few hours solo to my credit as well. When war broke out, I tried to enlist in the Royal Air Force, but they found out I was too young and it was a no go. Someday I'll wear RAF wings. At least I hope so—"

"Silence," the German lieutenant's harsh voice grated against my eardrums. "You will not speak."

"That bloke thinks he's a big shot," Barney whispered.

I smiled and nodded.

Our German transport continued to rumble and roll eastward. I was so tired I couldn't keep my eyes open anymore. I'd been through so much since this morning. It didn't take long for me to fall asleep.

The clanging gears and shouting and grating of German voices dragged me out of my sound slumber. Still dark out, but a faint light of a new dawn rose in the east. Our transport came to a stop in the center of a small village. Bombs and shells had devastated the area, but many buildings were still untouched. German soldiers in all kinds of uniforms were everywhere. A powerful hand slapped my shoulder. I twisted and looked into the small grey eyes of our German lieutenant.

"Wake up your friend," he snapped. "Get out, both of you."

"Where are we?" I asked and gently shook Barney, still fast asleep. "What town are we in, Lieutenant?"

The German officer smiled with a sly look on his face. I sensed the annoyance flashing as he blinked. He gripped Barney's shoulder and shook him savagely.

"Wake up, Englander," he shouted. "You had enough sleep, wake up." He slapped Barney across the cheek. My English friend woke up instantly and looked as if he was about to lunge at the German with a clenched fist when I grabbed his arm and pushed him back.

"Take it easy, Barney," I said. "This is the end of the line. We get off here. Are you okay?"

Barney shook his head and dug his knuckles into his sleep-filled eyes. In a few more seconds, he seemed to be fully awake. "Where are we? What is this place?"

The German lieutenant threw back his head and laughed. He wagged his finger in our faces. "You're at the headquarters of German Army Intelligence. I told you before, I'm taking you to the Kommandant. Now, we will learn all about you two. My advice is to answer all questions *Herr Kommandant* asks truthfully."

The lieutenant gave a curt nod and the Germans descended from the truck. They motioned for us to climb down and follow them.

The lieutenant pointed. "That building over there. Don't be foolish and try to run away. I warn you. You will be shot."

I shrugged and walked across the street to the doorway of a solidly built stone building. I glanced over my shoulder and saw Barney behind me. A guard standing in front clicked his heels and held his rifle at salute at the German lieutenant's approach.

The lieutenant barked an order in German and the guard saluted again. He executed a smart about-face and went in through the door. I got a quick glimpse of desks and chairs and part of a wall covered by an enormous map before the door slammed in my face. I looked at Barney and nodded and then glanced up into the small beady eyes of our German lieutenant.

"You will tell us the whole truth," the lieutenant said through his tightly clenched lips. "You'll do well to remember that."

The door opened, and the guard nodded at us. A soldier shoved me through the open door. "Get inside, get inside now."

4

After tripping over my feet through the open doorway, I shuffled in front of an enormous desk. At least nine feet long and five feet deep. It took up almost the entire side of the room. On it were papers, books, portable shortwave radio sets, and half a dozen telephones. A red-faced, bull-necked German wearing a staff colonel's uniform sat at the desk.

"*Herr Kommandant*, my prisoners," the lieutenant said. "*Heil Hitler.*"

The chunky German colonel lifted his gaze from the papers laid out in front of him. He looked at Barney and me, and I sensed the violence in him. Evilness dripped from every part of his body. After a long second of staring at us, he twisted his head toward the lieutenant.

"Is this a joke, *Herr Leutnant*?" he said in accented English and walked toward us. His booming voice shook the thick walls of the room. "Why have you brought me these peasants?" The German colonel lifted his finger the size of a banana and jabbed it at me. "Look at the clothes on that one —rags."

"They're not peasants, Herr Kommandant," the lieutenant said, his voice cracking. "This one here with the brown hair said he is American. The blonde-haired one is an Englishman. I caught them trying to sneak past our lines, driving an ambulance. They said they were lost and wanted to know the way to Courtrai. I caught them forty miles southeast of the city. I didn't believe them, and I escorted them here at once."

"What about the ambulance?" the colonel asked slowly. "Did you find wounded soldiers in it?"

"No, Herr Kommandant," the lieutenant said and shook his head. "There was nothing. It was empty. It seemed like it hadn't been used. That also added to my suspicion. On your orders, I will further examine the ambulance."

"Fine," the German colonel waved a dismissal with his hand.

"At once, Herr Kommandant," the lieutenant said in a syrupy voice. He thrust his arm forward in a Nazi salute and turned on his heels and stomped toward the door.

The colonel sat down behind his desk. He was quiet for a few moments while he stared at us. "What's all this about? How did you get so far behind our lines?"

"We told the truth to the lieutenant, sir," Barney said. "I was lost. It was all my fault. I had no idea where I was. You have no right to keep us here as prisoners. All we've done is got lost."

The German colonel's smile broadened, and his shoulders shook as he chuckled. The way his fat nose wobbled on his bull neck made him look like he had a pig's snout.

"I have no right, you say? I suppose you'll tell me all about it. Why you're here. What you're doing driving an ambulance?"

Barney paused for a moment before telling the story of how he left the Paris headquarters with the British Volunteer Ambulance Service. How he became separated from the others and of picking me up on the road.

"There you are, sir," Barney finished. "It was an unfortunate incident, and again, I've already told you it was my fault."

Colonel Snout shrugged. He began to speak but stopped. He swiveled around in his chair and gazed at the well-marked-up map that took up the wall behind him. Then he turned back to us and fixed his gaze on me.

"And you? Why were you forced to leave your car? And where is this French Army lieutenant?"

"I don't know where he is," I said. "When the German planes started shooting and bombing the poor refugees I—"

"Wait," the colonel snapped. "Our pilots don't shoot or bomb civilians. Those must've been French planes, or even British ones made up to look like German planes. Continue."

Anger welled up inside me. I saw those planes with my own eyes. I knew enough about foreign planes and they were not British or French. They were German. I was sure of it. My jaw dropped to hurl the lie back at the German colonel's face, then I thought better of it.

I explained, "Seventy miles north of Paris, I think, a few minutes before, we passed through a small village called Roye. I remember looking at my watch. It was a little after one in the afternoon."

"I see," Colonel Snout said in a whisper. He had an odd, confused look on his face. "And when you woke up, it was night? Saw this English boy's ambulance, and he picked you up?"

"That's right, sir," I said and nodded.

"And so," Colonel Snout said in the same tone, "a little while after one o'clock this afternoon, your friend picked you up and traveled over thirty miles—while unconscious? You expect me to believe that?"

"I'm not lying," I snapped. "You can believe what you want, but it's still the truth. I don't know how I got there. Maybe some car picked me up and then dumped me out thinking I was dead. Maybe somebody took me farther to rob me because of my American clothes. Maybe they'd thought I had some money and—"

I stopped short at the thought and searched the pockets of my torn clothes. I pulled out a handkerchief, broken pencil, and a bent penny I carried everywhere as my lucky piece. Everything else was gone: my wallet, my money, my passport—everything. I looked at Colonel Snout in an angry triumph.

"That must be what happened," I said in an excited voice. "Someone must've picked me up and robbed me. And then they left me in that field under the trees. And now I'm broke. I'll need money to get to England. I—"

I stopped short when the colonel smiled. This was a different kind of smile. A devilish smile with nothing pleasant about it: a tightlipped bitter smile. I shivered and felt the tingling of chicken skin all over my body.

"You're not going to England—yet," the colonel said. "Something is strange here, and I need to find out what."

"Why?" I blurted out. "We got lost in the dark, and that's all there is to it."

"He's right," Barney chimed in. "It's the truth. We're not even old enough to be soldiers yet."

Colonel Snout scowled. His heavy black brows formed a solid line across the lower part of his forehead. "Your sharp tongue may get you into more trouble than you think, my little English liar. You'd best take care to not lie to me. I have more questions. You both left Paris this morning? When? Did you see French troops and tanks and other things on the march?"

"I saw millions of them," Barney answered. "And airplanes too. I never saw so many soldiers and so much military equipment in my life."

"So?" The colonel let out a long breath. "You must've seen which way they were heading, of course?"

"Naturally," Barney said. "They're heading into Belgium, of course. And not just French troops with tanks and guns. Thousands of British and Canadians with thousands more from Australia, New Zealand, and South Africa. The sky was filled with RAF planes and French planes and—"

Colonel Snout's booming laughter stopped Barney in his tracks. The fat German shook like jelly and blew his nose before continuing. "I admire you, young Englander. I think now I should be very frightened and order a general retreat of German troops at once, eh?"

"You'll be forced to, shortly," Barney said.

The colonel's face turned severe, and his laughter faded. "Germans will never hear an order like that because it's never given." The colonel raised his voice. "But I see you want to treat this as a joke?"

"Do you expect us to give you military information?" I said.

"It would help you, perhaps even save your life. You want to return to England, eh?"

"Not as traitors, we don't." I puffed my chest out. "I won't answer questions about military information, even if I had any to give you."

"Good on you, mate," Barney said in a low voice. "He won't make bloody traitors out of us."

I stood with my shoulders back, my head up, and masked my face with the most defiant look I could muster. Colonel Snout glared back for a moment. Then the corners of his lips pulled back, and he smiled.

"I like you more for refusing. If I was in your shoes, I wouldn't say anything either, even if I happened to get captured. Alright, we'll speak no more about this. But I must make a report. I need your names and addresses. I will send word through the Red Cross to your families, so they will know where you are."

"I live in America," I said, "but my father's in London like I told you, I don't know where."

"What's his name?" The German colonel picked up a

pencil. "I'll have word sent to the hotel where you stayed in Paris. It'll be forwarded to him wherever he is."

I hesitated for a moment. Then I decided there was nothing else that could be done. "Douglas C. Archer. My name is John Archer. We were at Hotel de Ney, Twenty-One Rue Passey, Paris."

That little bit of information startled Colonel Snout. He gave me a long, piercing look and then scribbled something onto a piece of paper in front of him. Then he glanced up at Barney.

"And you?"

"My name is Barney James. I live at ninety-seven Baker Street in London. But look here, sir. You don't really intend to keep us, prisoners, do you? I mean, after everything you know."

Colonel Snout laughed and shook his head. "Keep you prisoners? Of course not. But I can't let you go until I get proof of who you are, now can I? In a short time, I'll know if you told me the truth or not. And if you have, I'll put you in a car and pass you through the Belgian lines."

"We have told you the truth," Barney said in a voice dripping with annoyance.

"Then there's nothing for you to worry about," the colonel said. "And now you're probably hungry? I'll make sure you two are taken care of and given something to eat."

Colonel Snout jabbed a button on the desk with his thick finger. As if by magic, a side door swung open, and a German soldier popped into the room. The colonel fired words in German to him so fast—they sounded like a low guttural growl. The soldier saluted and motioned for us to walk out ahead of him. Once he closed the door, he pointed toward a flight of stairs. The soldier stopped us on the second landing, pushed open a door, and waved us inside. Two army cots with a blanket for each and a couple of broken chairs were all that greeted us. A single window in the rear of the room glowed from the moonlight a good five feet up from the floor. It was thick with cobwebs and dust and looked like it hadn't been opened in years.

I looked at Barney and then around the room again. I heard the click of the door latch and then the grating sound of the bolt being shot home. I jumped for the door and grabbed hold of the knob. It turned in my hand, but the door would not open. I gulped and put my foot against the wall and tried to yank it open. No luck. I looked back at Barney, his face had paled, but his eyes were still flaming with defiance.

5

"KEEP YOUR CHIN UP, BARNEY," I said. "They can't do anything to us. They wouldn't dare."

Barney lifted his face and nodded. Not even the faintest suggestion of defeat shone in his eyes. "I'm not afraid of them. I'm angry at myself. I could kick myself all around this room. Because of my own stupidity, I've gone and now lost a perfectly good ambulance. That's what I'm bloody mad about. Now it's fallen into the hands of the Germans. I'm just no good, Archer."

"Knock it off. You were good downstairs. You got right back at him when I was standing there quaking in my boots. Don't worry about the ambulance. We'll get it back. Maybe even steal it back."

Barney's eyes lit up with a bright flicker of hope.

"You think so, Archer? You think there's a chance we can get out of this?"

"We can try. You just gotta keep yourself under control and—wait. Someone's coming up the stairs. Barney, we can't let them think we're worried or scared in the least."

"Right, mate," Barney whispered. "You can count on me to hold up my end."

Footsteps were outside the door. The outside bolt slid back, and the door creaked open. A German guard stood in the hallway outside. In one hand he carried a battered, rickety tray with bread and sausages, and the other one was a bundle of old clothes. Colonel Snout stood behind him. The colonel's fat face beamed in the glow from the moonlit window.

"Think I've forgotten you?" He strode into the room. "Of course I haven't. Here's some food and fresh clothes. I'll have what you're wearing mended, and all cleaned up."

"How kind of you, Colonel," Barney said in a mocking tone. "You'll be disappointed, though."

"Disappointed?" The German colonel gave Barney a puzzled look.

"Yes, I'm afraid so." Barney peeled off his dirt and dust-caked clothes. "You won't find secret messages or maps sown into the lining. No matter what you suspect, we are not bloody spies."

Colonel Snout laughed again, but a look in his eyes didn't signal laughter to me. The German colonel obviously didn't like the fact that a seventeen-year-old English boy could see right through him.

"That's ridiculous," the colonel said. "Of course you're not spies. I just want to have your clothes cleaned. We Germans take good care of the people we protect. You'll do well to think of that when you return to your homelands. Now take your clean clothes and eat."

Colonel Snout waited until the guard gathered up our clothes, then smiled at us before turning on his heels and leaving the room, followed by the guard. I waited until the door bolt was jammed home, and then half-starved, I started to devour my tray of fresh-baked bread and juicy sausages. From the very first mouthful, it was a delightful surprise: excellent food and plenty of it.

We started to wolf down our food like desperate refugees who hadn't eaten in days. Then I stopped, still chewing on a sausage, and spit it back onto the tray. I put my hand on Barney's shoulder. "Wait, this could be a trick."

"What's that, mate?" Barney said and opened his mouth, sausage dangling. "You think they're trying to poison us? I did once hear a story about Germans using some kind of drug to make people talk. But Archer, I'm starving."

"Me too," I said. "That's not what I mean, though. I'm sure the food's okay. It's the point. I bet the troops don't get this kind of food. I've got a hunch he wants to make a point. Feed us up good, so we'll talk about the French and British military units we saw yesterday."

Barney snorted. "Then he's a bloody fool. If he thinks filling my stomach with food will make me tell him anything."

"Same for me, but what I mean is this: I think it'll be smart if we didn't eat all this food. Let's save some. At least the bread. We might need it later and—"

"Who appointed you Winston Churchill?" Barney made a point to slowly stuff another piece of bread in his mouth. "I'm not sure I like you giving me orders. I should be the one giving the orders and making the bloody plans around here."

I groaned. "Alright, go ahead and tell me your plan on how we escape."

"Escape?" Barney set his tray of bread and sausages down on the cot.

"Isn't that our duty?" I said. "Shouldn't we resist and try to escape?"

"I thought this wasn't your war, mate. I thought you were here for a Paris vacation, and you wanted no part of all this?"

"I *don't* want any part of this. But I don't want to stay here as a prisoner, either."

Barney gave his tray of food a last, long look before pushing it farther away. "Then that's what we have to do—escape. And when we do, we'll need some food to take along.

I nodded but said nothing. An uneasy feeling rose inside of me, and the back of my neck tingled. A sure sign that trouble was ahead. We may have Colonel Snout confused about who we really are. He can't really believe we're spies. But how can I know for sure? The Germans hope to drain us of any information we can tell them. Colonel Snout will keep us prisoners here until satisfied. Maybe even keep us as prisoners long after. Would they ever let us pass safely through the Belgian lines, knowing full well we'd tell the authorities what we'd seen on the German side?

Never. My hunger disappeared. I got up and walked over toward the window. The sill was up to my chin, and I tried to focus outside into the moonlit night. I wiped away the dust and cobwebs with my palm, and what I saw brought no joy. The window looked out onto a tree-studded hill that blocked everything beyond. The waxing moon revealed cluster after cluster of planes in V formations. All flying swiftly westward. I strained my ears to barely catch the throbbing beat of German engines. As those sounds faded, I heard louder and more thunderous noises farther to the west. German bombers were once again dropping their loads of death and destruction on the soldiers and civilians of the country Adolf Hitler crushed under his iron heel.

I turned from the window and stared at nothing. I'd only been seventeen for a few months, but today I felt at least a dozen years older. What was it that I'd seen since leaving Paris that added years to my thinking if not my body? I still felt fierce anger at the injustices I'd seen since yesterday. I want to do something about it. But what? Fight the Nazis by myself? Or with Barney? This blazing desire burned inside and urged me to do what I can to help.

"What you thinking about Archer?" Barney asked, breaking me out of my daydream.

I paused and used the knuckle of my finger to rub my temple. "I might be crazy, but I want the chance to actually do something. I want a chance to get back at the Germans for what they've done. We're too young to enlist, but there must be something we can do. I want to do it."

"So now you want to fight?" Barney asked.

"Do you have any other dumb questions?"

Barney shook his head. "I'm glad you've come to your senses, mate."

"Do you have any idea where we are? I've never been to Belgium before. I think we're still in Belgium, right?"

Barney stuck his forehead to the window. "From the looks of the buildings and some townsfolk we saw when we arrived, I'd think so. But what town we're in, I don't have any bloody idea. I . . ."

"What's the matter?"

"Wait. That map in the colonel's office downstairs. Did you see it? And see how it was marked with those little pins and tiny flags?" Barney said with a broad smile.

"Yeah, I guess," I said. "But I didn't give it much attention."

"Me neither," Barney said. "But mate, we're at an intelligence headquarters, and I bet those little pins and flags are the points marked for the advance of the German forces. See what I mean? If we could get a good look at that map, and at least remember some of the things it tells, and then if we could escape from here, we could . . ."

Barney drifted off. He was shaking from eager excitement. I grabbed him by both shoulders. "Barney, you're right. We could tell the Allied commanders where some of the German units are and where they're heading. We need to figure out how we can get another look at that map."

"What if we went and pounded on the bloody door. We'll tell the Kraut soldier to get Colonel Snout. We'll pretend to tell him everything we know if he'll let us go. I'll bet he'll at least take us down to his office to hear what we have to say."

"Maybe," I said. "But it's too soon to make him think we're scared and giving up. Besides, maybe he's not really tricking us. Maybe he really is going to just check on us and let us go."

"What? C'mon mate, you think he's going to let us go back and tell anyone what we've seen behind the German lines?" Barney said. "No chance, Archer. You gotta be off your topper."

I chuckled. "Yeah, you're right. He's not going to let us go. Even if he thinks we're just caught up in the wrong place at the wrong time."

Barney sat across from me on his cot with his arms crossed, nodding like an eager dog waiting for a bone.

"Only one thing left for us to do," I continued. "We can't try to escape now in broad daylight. Let's put on these clothes and catch up on some sleep. All we can do now is wait for a while. Wait to see what his next move is."

"I hate waiting," Barney pulled on the rest of the clothes the guard had brought. "But I agree, Archer. There's nothing else we can do right now."

I flung myself down on the cot and put my palms behind the back of my head. "We'll have plenty to do later on. Wait and see Barney. Just wait and see."

I was in the middle of a good deep sleep when I heard the clinking and clanking of keys in the lock as our door creaked open. A German guard shouted and waved for us to follow him downstairs. Looks like Colonel Snout's going to make the next move. We followed the guard down the steps and were led back to the colonel's office, where he waited behind his desk.

"Have a seat," the colonel said, making an expansive gesture with his wrist. "I want to talk to you again."

I glanced at Barney and then sat down as ordered, slowly. I felt something in the air was wrong. My heart raced. The invisible hairs on the back of my neck began to stick up, and my palms sweated, getting clammy and cold.

Colonel Snout leaned forward and clasped his big hands together on the edge of his desk. "Our leader is a man of peace. He loves peace and would gladly give his life for peace among nations." He pointed at Barney. "You English, did the Führer declare war on your country? Or on France? No. Your countries declared war on us, Germany. Listen, don't you want peace?"

"Of course," Barney said. Then a mischievous smile appeared across his face. ". . . at the right time."

"No!" The colonel slammed his ham-sized fist down on the table. "We want peace as soon as possible. Now is the best time before there's any more bloodshed. You, two young men, can help bring this war to an early end. You'll be doing a favor for Germany's enemies. Now, why don't you tell me the truth. And then everything will be fine."

Neither of us said a word. It felt like I was listening to a broken record. All I heard echoing through my head was *tell me the truth, tell me the truth, tell me the truth*, like the title of the same boring song I'd heard ten times before. I sat there with my mouth shut and my eyes fixed on the massive map hung on the wall. I tried to memorize where the pins and the flags were, and the towns' and cities' names on the locations. One town on the map was smudged by a finger with some marks. It was named Stalin and close to the Belgian-German frontier. I had a hunch that was precisely where we were. Close to the German border. But how far behind German lines? I thought of that long ride in the motorized transport last night, and my heart sank to my knees.

"Well, for the last time," Colonel Snout said in a thundering voice. "Are you going to tell me the truth?"

Barney shot to his feet. "We already have. We told you the same thing—the truth. Over a dozen times. What more do you have to hear to believe us?"

The colonel slammed his hands down flat on the desk, and hoisted his huge bulk forward, and glared at us.

"I've tried to be kind and fair with you both. Since you refuse my kindness, I must now treat you as my enemy. I will have you both shot."

6

Shot?

My mouth gaped open, and I stared at Colonel Snout, waiting for him to burst into laughter. The German colonel did not laugh. He leaned forward over the desk and stared at me with his beady eyes that looked like twin ice cubes.

"You can't shoot us," I said. "We haven't done anything."

"He's bluffing," Barney said. "This is all just a bluff."

"A bluff?" Colonel Snout snarled. "You think I'm a fool? I never bluff." The colonel held up a map in his hand.

"So what?" I said. "I don't know that map. I've never seen it before." I looked over at Barney, and he shrugged his shoulders.

"It was found under the seat of your ambulance." Colonel Snout said in a flat voice that made me shiver. "There are marks on it. Numbers and figures written in pencil near the names of towns you passed before you were caught."

The colonel took a deep breath.

"Have you told me the truth? No, you lied. This map contains information that would be useful to Germany's enemies. You thought you could protect yourselves by driving an ambulance? Wrong. But you can save your lives now by listening to what I have to say."

I considered trying to say something, but my tongue was stuck to the roof of my mouth. My knees were going weak and my stomach churned. I focused on standing still and upright. Was this all a crazy dream? A nightmare? In a few minutes, was I gonna wake up and find myself safe and sound in my hotel in Paris? I've never seen this map before. I know nothing about a map.

I twisted my gaze over to Barney. He stood there a little paler, but with a firm chin, his eyes filled with scorn and defiance.

"I don't have any idea what you're talking about," Barney said. "Like I told you, I was taking the ambulance to Courtrai. And for the hundredth time, I lost my way."

Colonel Snout flicked his wrist in an exaggerated movement, like he was brushing Barney's words to the side. "Enough lies. This is a serious offense. Perhaps you did not collect information about our advance units. Perhaps you are only taking it to someone else. Yes, perhaps you didn't even know you were being used for such a task."

I took a step toward the colonel, and he waved me off before I could talk.

"Let's say that's true," the colonel continued. "This information was found on you, and that is serious. To avoid being treated as spies, you must answer the questions I ask you."

"What questions?" Barney asked.

Colonel Snout smiled and the stern look faded from his face. "Better." He spread the map out on the desk. "Here, you've marked a line showing the route you traveled from Paris. Each town you passed is marked. Those towns are French troops and equipment garrisons. This town here close to the Belgian border. What did you see there? British troops? French troops? What was their equipment? Tanks? Big ones, small ones? Were there motorized antiaircraft batteries? Were there—"

The colonel stopped and looked up from the map. "Are you listening to me?"

"Of course I'm listening," Barney said. "But I'm not answering any of these bloody questions, even if you do shoot me." Barney licked his lips and then put his shoulders back and stiffened up a bit more.

I shook my head and smiled. Barney had that cool, calm courage, which made the English famous all over the world. This situation was starting to head south quick. I turned to face Colonel Snout. "We're not saying a thing," I shouted. "I demand to see the American consul. *Now*."

Colonel Snout stared at Barney. He ignored me, treated me like I hadn't even spoken. For a few long moments, he continued to stare and then sighed. The colonel raised both of his hands in a gesture dripping with despair. "Very well. That's all I have now. I'll give you until tomorrow morning to think it over—and change your mind—*Hüten*."

The side door popped open and another guard appeared. Colonel Snout pointed a finger at us. In English, he said, "Take them back. And stand guard outside the door. If either of them tries to escape—shoot them."

The colonel gave us an angry stare and a curt nod, then busied himself with papers on his desk. After we were back in our prison room, the door was closed and bolted. I listened to the clacking of hobnailed boots as the guard paced up and down the hallway outside.

Barney sat on his cot across from me and shivered. I said, "He was bluffing. He'd never shoot us. I'll make him let me see the American consul. I'll make him let me call the American ambassador in Brussels."

"I hope you do for your sake, mate. But England's at war, and I'm an Englishman. And Archer. . . that map was mine. I used it to mark my route until it got too dark."

It felt like fingers of ice clutched at my heart and pressed. I sucked air sharply into my lungs. "Wait, so you did write down all that stuff he was talking about?"

"Oh no, not that. I just penciled in the route I'd taken until it got too dark. After that, I lost my pencil when I tried to mark it in the glow of the dash light. The rest he must've marked himself."

"I don't understand. Why?"

"Look Archer," Barney said, "they did it to scare us and make us answer questions. They're going to hold a military court and use that map as evidence. They're going to try to scare us into talking. I knew a Jewish boy in England who escaped with his family from the Gestapo."

Barney leaned forward on his cot. He had a burning, piercing look in his eyes. "He told me about the tricks they play to scare you into telling them things. That's what they plan to do with us. But I won't tell them anything—nothing. Yes, it's my map. So what? They won't frighten me into telling them any bloody thing that could hurt the Allies. They cannot make me."

"You bet they can't," I said. "They won't get anything from me either."

We sat in silence on our cots, lost in our own thoughts. The only noise was the clicking of the German soldier's boots outside and the beating of my own heart. I shook my head to get rid of the thoughts of what it would feel like to get shot and die from a firing squad. It scared me, but what worried me more was what would happen to my new pal, Barney.

"I don't think they're going to hurt you, Archer," Barney said. "Just keep asking to see the American consul. You're an American. You'll be alright."

"Yeah maybe, but what about you?"

"I won't tell them a bloody thing, no matter what they do to me," Barney said with a crooked smile.

I opened my mouth to speak and then checked myself. I

stood up and walked to the corner of the room and spun toward Barney. "So that's the kind of pal you are then, huh? Just up and let me down like this?"

Barney jerked his head up. "Let you down, mate? What the bloody—"

"Yeah, let me down," I snapped. I felt heat rising in my stomach and spreading throughout my body. "Aren't we pals? I thought we were gonna see this through together?"

"But Archer, you—"

"What, walk out and leave you behind?" I interrupted him. "Quit a pal just like that because I'm an American and you're English? No chance. We're sticking together."

"Look Archer, I got you into this mess. I was only thinking of—"

In a flash, the anger washed out of my body. I grinned at my pal. "I'll get you out. We've got until tomorrow morning to think this through. Wait . . . we're done thinking about things. It's time to start doing things. Are you game, Barney?"

He answered by putting out his hand. When we clasped them. I felt a sliver of hope slide through me as the color returned to Barney's face.

"I saw something besides airplanes at the window a while ago." I nodded at him. "I want to show you."

Barney followed me toward the window. "Look down," I whispered. "See? The bottom half of this building sticks out from the roof. It can't be over six feet under this window. And not more than ten feet from the edge of the roof to the backyard. Think you could jump it?"

"Sure. But what about this window, here? It's screwed in." Barney rattled the base of the window.

I pulled an army canteen spoon from the pocket of my new clothes. "Got all that figured out. I swiped this from the breakfast tray. I had a hunch and stuck it in my pocket. Spoons can make good screwdrivers."

I slipped the tip of the spoon handle into the groove of the nearest screw and pressed down with both hands. I turned the screw one-sixteenth of an inch or so and then stopped. "Good. I was scared it'd be so rusted it wouldn't budge." I turned back to Barney. "Looks like it'll work. Go over to the door and start talking to me really loud. Talk about anything. Let's talk about baseball."

"I'm English. I don't know anything about baseball."

"Good point. Too bad I don't know diddly about Cricket. Just ask me questions about baseball, and I'll give you answers," I lowered my voice to a whisper, "but keep an open ear out for that guard. If he starts to open the door, ask me, 'What's a home run?' Then, I'll know to get away from the window."

Barney chuckled. "You're a devious one, aren't you, Archer."

I smiled. Am I devious? Maybe determined, determined to get out of this mess. Determined to get some payback at the Nazis for ruining my trip to Paris. And most of all, for killing so many innocent people. I can't let that stand.

As soon as Barney was over by the door, I gave my full attention to the first screw. Lucky for us, the window was so dirty that no one could see what I was doing from the outside.

Barney jabbered question after question about baseball, and I automatically answered them. I worked with the tip of the spoon on the screws. Eight of them. It must've been well over an hour before I had seven of them out. I loosened the eighth one and let it stay partly in the hole so the window would remain in place. I took little pieces of cobweb and covered the screw holes so no one would notice. Then I walked over to my small army cot and sat down.

"Right then, that's enough about baseball." Barney said in a booming voice, winking. "Looks like we're not to get any food tonight. I guess I'll try to get some sleep then." Barney stretched out on his cot.

I pointed at the window and smirked.

7

Somewhere off in the distance, a church clock rang. I slowly sat up on my cot and counted ten strokes. A light glow from the moon gave an eerie shadow in our dark and dank cell. I sat there, listening for any sounds.

The guard outside in the hallway coughed and struck a match. Muffled sounds of hobnailed boots marched along the street outside. The clanking sound of tanks and scout car tractor treads on the stones. An occasional dull boom of heavy guns or exploding bombs, and even the sound of planes droning high up in the night sky.

I held my breath while I listened. I also listened for another sound. One I could feel as well as hear: the pounding of my own heart. My chest ached, my throat was bone dry from the excitement and suspense of what was to happen next. For the last few hours, Barney and I remained stretched out motionless on the cots. Every second lasted a minute, every minute an hour and so on until eternity. I restrained myself from leaping to my feet and shouting at the top of my lungs. I was shaking with excitement and the pent up frustration of *waiting, waiting, waiting.*

Three or four times, that guard opened our door and played

with the beam of his flashlight. The first time Colonel Snout was with him, I could recognize his voice even in German. He muttered something and then left, clomping down the stairs.

I couldn't stand waiting around anymore. It was like every fiber in my whole being screamed for action. I'd waited long enough to make our captors believe that they were done for the night. Only a couple minutes ago, the guard had taken another look. It was time to do this. Now or never.

I slipped off my cot as quietly as I could. I crept over to Barney. I held one hand, ready to clasp it over his mouth in case he woke with a yell. I whispered in his ear. "Barney, wake up." I shook him gently with my other hand.

"I'm awake Archer. Are we ready?"

"Yep. The guard won't be back in here for a few minutes. You get any sleep?"

"Until you woke me up, I was dreaming of a pint in a pub." Barney's face creased, and his good humor faded. His voice had a serious tone. "Look Archer, sure you don't want to change your mind? I can have a go at this alone. I'll understand. You could still have a way out with the American consul. They'll come looking for us, you know."

"Not a chance," I said. "Now, pipe down and take off your shoes. We can't risk making any sounds. That guard may have big ears."

We crept across the small room to the window. I took out my spoon slash screwdriver and went to work on that last screw. The instant the last screw was out, I tried to pry the frame out with my fingers. It wouldn't budge. I sucked in air to my achy lungs and worked the end of the spoon into the side crack as a lever. The window still didn't move. My heart sank as I felt the spoon bending underneath my hand.

"What's the matter?" Barney whispered.

"It's stuck. Swollen from the weather."

The light from the moon had faded. It was dark. So dark I

could hardly see. The church clock rang three strokes. We had to hurry. I ran my hand over the window frame—a nail head at the bottom. I didn't see it, but I could feel it. A thin one. Maybe the window will slide over it.

For two long minutes, I worked on that nail pressed flat on the base of the board of the sill. I pressed down with the spoon again. The window began to move. My face was wet with salty, nervous sweat. My body trembled. I could hardly control my wrist from making the spoon click against the windowsill. I fought back my fear and nervousness. I focused on getting this task done. Finally, I'd worked out the window enough so I could get my fingers under a corner. From there, I yanked out the entire frame, but a corner of it caught on a splintered sliver of the sill. The sliver snapped off like a pistol shot. I froze. My ears strained for the sounds of the guard in the hallway.

No click of the bolt or rattling of the latch. I slowly released the air from my lungs. I lowered the window frame down onto the floor to the side where we would be sure not to hit when we climbed out the window.

I grabbed Barney's arm. "You go first. I'll make a step with my hands. Put your foot in and I'll boost you up."

I crouched down and laced my fingers together with the palms facing upward to form a step. Barney put one foot in it and one hand on my shoulder to steady himself. I slowly boosted him up the wall. As soon as he had half his body through the open square window, he released the pressure from his foot on my locked hands. He squirmed up the rest of the way like a snake.

"Get your feet out and then let yourself down by your hands," I whispered. "The roof shouldn't be more than a few inches on your toes. Watch out. It slants down a bit."

"I'll be alright, mate." Barney twisted around on the sill, hanging on his stomach. "Can you make it down alone?"

"Don't wait for me," I whispered. "Just sneak down the roof and drop to the ground. I'll be right behind you."

I waited until I heard the soft thud of Barney's feet hitting the roof. I grabbed hold of the sill with my hands and hoisted my body upward. I sat poised on the sill, grinning into the darkened room. Then I swiveled over and lowered myself down. I felt like a cat gently crawling down this sloping roof. I pressed flat on my stomach and stuck my head over the edge of the roof. Below me was nothing but a sea of inky darkness. For some reason, I froze with a twinge of panic shooting through my body.

"Barney?" I whispered.

"I'm here, Archer. On the ground to the left. All clear down here. Soft ground. Come on down."

I twisted over and let myself down, following the sound of Barney's voice. When my feet touched the ground, I felt a hand on my arm.

"Well, there goes the first part," Barney whispered. "What's the next move?"

"Our shoes," I said and pulled them down to the ground. "Then we head straight up that hill there and keep going north."

"North?" Barney said in a puzzled whisper. "Why don't we head west towards the Belgian lines? I got a good look at that map. I think—"

A shaft of yellow light cut through the darkness. I froze, and we backed up against the rear wall of the building. My heart jumped into my throat. I waited in fear for that shaft of light to sweep over and reveal us in its glow. My taut nerves twanged like plucked fiddle strings. Then I realized someone had turned a light on inside the building against where we crouched. The shaft of light had been inside, light flooding out through a rear window. It shined at the bottom of the hill slope a dozen yards away. I had this sudden insane crazy desire to burst out laughing.

"That scared the bloody hell out of me," Barney said, gasping.

"Talk later," I said. "We need to make tracks. Got your shoes on?"

"Right. You lead Archer. I'm behind you."

I reached the corner and stopped. I peered around it, hoping that Lady Luck was with me. I half expected to be looking down an alley to the street out front. But it wasn't an alley. It was a small courtyard that connected to the next building. It had a high fence in the front blocked off by a view of the street. I couldn't see the road, but when we started up the hill slope, there were no passing soldiers that could see us.

"Stay close Barney," I whispered over my shoulder. "We are going to make for the top of that hill there."

I bent down low and turned a sharp left. I scuttled across thirty feet of bare ground and dove into the shrubs that fringed the base of the hill. I had my hands out in front to not slam straight into a tree. We trotted up the slope as fast as we could. By the time I was halfway up, my breath came in wicked gasps, and my legs felt like withered sticks that could snap at any second.

I gritted my teeth and called down for every ounce of strength in my body. This was tougher going than I'd thought. From the prison room window, the hill slope looked like it wasn't that steep. But now, climbing it in the dark, dodging tree trunks and jutting rocks, it seemed to rise straight up in front of me. Every so often, I twisted around to make sure Barney was still with me. And every time, he was right behind me. At my heels, puffing and panting and stuck to me like a wet sock.

I refused to allow myself a rest, even for a moment. Barney wasn't complaining, and if he could take it, so could I. Even though Barney was shorter and weighed less, he had a strong fighting spirit and courage in his heart. I kept climbing on and on and on through the black night until we reached the crest. I staggered along the flat crest for a few yards and sank down into the soft earth. Barney plopped down next to me. For several minutes, only the sounds of our labored breathing broke the silence.

I pushed myself up to a sitting position and wiped the dripping sweat off my face with the sleeve of my shirt. "Guess I'm out of shape for track. That was tough. I didn't think we'd ever make it. You okay, Barney?"

My English friend groaned as he sat up. "I guess," he sucked in great gulps of cool night air. "I hope we don't have to keep doing that, though."

Barney leaned back onto the ground and stretched out. "Can't see much from up here. They're probably not taking chances on showing lights in case bombers come over. I'd love to see a big bomb drop on Colonel Snout's intelligence office. He deserves it."

I snickered louder than I meant to but felt much better.

We stared into the town from the crest. Less than a couple dozen lights were showing, and at least half of them were the dim lights of army cars and trucks moving along the town's main street.

"About that map," I said in a low voice. "I can't figure out how far we are away from the Belgian lines. It can't be that far. They just started the invasion yesterday morning, so they couldn't have gone that far into the country yet."

"I don't think so, mate. I heard the Germans made ninety miles a day with the *blitzkrieg* through Poland. My father taught me a lot about marking army maps. Of course, I don't know what all those markings meant on the colonel's map. But I'm sure those little yellow pins were their most advanced units."

"Then they could be as far west as Brussels and Charleroi.

That's miles away. What about the Belgian frontier forts? They must've been able to hold them back?"

"I don't know, Archer. I bet the Germans are doing the same thing they did against the Polish. They're using their light and fast mobile units to scoot around past the heavily fortified centers and capturing small positions in the rear. Then the bombers and heavy attack tanks would have a go at the big forts. Like my father said shortly after the Polish invasion, you don't fight with trench warfare anymore. It's all about *blitzkrieg* nowadays. A lightning attack with small, fast units, the main body moving up behind and concentrating on the main points of defense."

"You sound like a military expert," I said. "How do you know so—"

"And don't forget about the *Luftwaffe*," Barney continued, not even realizing he cut me off. "It cleared the way for him in Poland and in Denmark and Norway. Hitler's doing the same thing against the Belgians. That's at least until we stop them. And we will bloody stop them, don't you worry."

"Okay, got it," I said, finally able to get a word in. "This war is going to be different from the last. But look, there were some blue pins on that map in Colonel Snout's office, and beside each one of them was a date. I saw dates a week and two weeks from now. And there were blue pins all the way across Belgium to the English Channel. That must mean . . . the yellow pins show where the Germans are today and the blue pins mark places they expect to capture. Is that true? What do you think?"

"We've seen something the Allied high command would pay millions of pounds to see. We had access to an intelligence map of the whole German plan of invasion. I'm sure of it."

I jumped to my feet. "Then let's go. We've got to find the Allied high command—wherever they are. We can't show them the map, but between us we should remember enough about it to help plenty, we can—"

A wild yell from the base of the hill followed by three pistol shots cut through the night air. I looked down the hill and saw a cluster of lights spring into action. I was sure they came from the building where we had been held. Seconds later, more shots and shouting. The guard probably took another look and found out we'd escaped. Now that the alarm was sounded, I felt like a fool for wasting all this time talking. I grabbed Barney and pulled him up to his feet.

"We gotta go. Fast. Stay close to me. We can still head north."

"Archer, why north? We need to go west. Belgium is west."

"No, we're going north," I said in a harsher tone than I meant. "Look, the Germans must think we're gonna try to go west to reach the Belgian lines. They will expect us and send word ahead and hunt us toward the west. If we go north, we'll fool them. At least, I hope. It's our best bet." I pointed toward the road. "Look, army cars are already heading west. Come on, let's go."

8

I COULDN'T TAKE another step. Dawn must be coming soon. We trudged across this strange country through the darkness. Trying to put more ground between the Germans and us. We stumbled past and hid from roving German mop-up patrols. We'd crouch for an hour in a road ditch while a long line of tanks and artillery rumbled past, heading west.

I didn't care if the whole German Army was at my heels. I was going to stop and rest. I reached the limit of my endurance. Barney and I had proven ourselves to be men during our mad flight across enemy-held ground. Where were we? We followed the North Star the whole way. We were forced to change direction to skirt around bomb blasted villages filled with German troops and roads clogged with the Nazi war machine. It was impossible to guess how far we'd gone or even in what direction.

We stood in an outer edge of a dew-covered woods and spotted the shadowy shapes of barren fields beyond. I flung myself down under prickly bushes and gave my body over to utter fatigue. This wariness had fought to drag me down for the last several miles. My throat was like sandpaper. I craved water. My stomach snarled for more of that bread and sausage we'd saved and stuffed inside our shirts before crawling out the window. I blinked and that smell of fresh baked bread and juicy sausages gave me hope, but they would have to wait until later. I was too tired now. I remember Barney flopping down next to me in a dreamlike way, and seconds later slipping into a blissful sleep.

A soothing warmth on my back woke me. I tried to move, but the aches and pains rippling through my body made me stifle a groan. I stayed where I was, my face buried in my crossed arms, soaking up the gentle heat on my back. I rolled over and stared up through the bush branches at the sky—another perfect spring day. The sun was well up on high. Then my tired brain clicked, and I sat bolt upright.

"It must be close to noon," I said. "We still got a long way to go. But where? In what direction?"

I turned to shake sleeping Barney next to me, but I didn't have the heart to wake him when I saw his pale, drawn face. My English friend was dead to the world. One look at the exhausted expression on his face told me he would not be fit to travel, even if awake. Was it dangerous to stay where we were? German soldiers could stumble on us at any moment. But a strange sense of responsibility washed over me. By more or less our mutual consent, I had become the leader. And a leader needs to use his head. I wouldn't be using my head to wake up Barney and force this poor kid to keep moving on.

"It's best to stick here, at least until dark," I argued with myself. "Plus, we're pretty well hidden up under these bushes. And I haven't got the heart to wake you right now."

I put my hand inside my shirt and pulled out half of my crushed loaf of bread and a piece of sweaty sausage. I nibbled on a little of both and then forced myself to put the rest back into my shirt. My grumbling stomach ached for more, and I was now even thirstier. I'd rather have a cool glass of water to quench my thirst right now than have the opportunity to stick a bayonet in Hitler's chest.

I laid back on the ground and started thinking about Paris and Audrey. Anything to take my mind off present circumstances. But after a couple seconds, it was no use. I sat up and looked around. I spotted a farmhouse a half-mile away. Smoke wafted from the farmhouse's chimney. Figures moved around in the yard. The sun glaring in my eyes made it hard to tell if they were German troops. A moving cloud of dust blowing in circles signaled a car traveling down the road to the right. The car came into view from behind a string of trees. It drove up to the farmhouse and then came to a stop. Four men climbed out and hurried into the farmhouse. My faint hope flickered out at once. I strained to make out the bucket-shaped helmets and the tight-fitting field grey uniforms of German officers.

Trying to approach the farmhouse was out of the question. I'd hoped they were peasant farmers. But that was not to be. This place was alive with Hitler's soldiers. Fighting back my momentary defeat, I slowly got to my feet and made sure Barney was still asleep. I crept off into the woods in search of a creek or small pond.

I broke branches off bushes every now and then so I could find my way back. At the end of a quarter-mile in, the ground sloped into a shallow valley with a small creek trickling through. I rushed down to it and flung flat on the ground, burying my face in the icy cold water. Never in my life had anything tasted so good, so completely satisfying as the coolness of that creek. I cupped my hands and drank like a camel in a desert oasis. Then I tore off part of my shirtsleeves and used it to wash my face and neck. I felt like a fresh man and retraced my steps back to my hiding place.

Barney was awake when I got back. He looked like a scared, ragged cat. "What in the bloody hell, mate? When I woke up, I couldn't remember if we came to this spot together or if we lost each other. I came close to yelling out for you and then saw those bloody Germans at that farmhouse. Where have you been? Where are we?"

"I wish I knew. But there's a creek about a quarter of a mile in. In case you'd like a long drink of cold water?"

"I'd say so." Barney jumped to his feet. "My throat feels like it's full of dust."

I pointed down toward the creek. "You'll see branches broken off the bushes. I'll wait here and figure out our next move."

Barney nodded and hurried off down into the woods.

I sat on the ground cross-legged and fixed my eyes on that farmhouse. Last night in our prison room, my brain concentrated on that one problem—getting out of that room. Now that we've escaped and put a lot of distance from there, we still have more problems to confront and consider. First off, we need to figure out where we are. Then we need to decide whether it is safe to head west or continue north. And then the problem of food. Whatever direction we go: we face a long road. And our little bit of bread and sausage would not last forever. We needed food . . . and that farmhouse looked like our best option.

My thoughts trailed off as Barney came up and sat next to me. He looked like a different person. His eyes sparkled, not heavy with fatigue. Color returned to his face. He had a satisfied, radiant smile on his lips.

"I'll remember that creek for the rest of my life," Barney said. "Water never tasted so good. Have you dreamed up a plan yet? I hope you don't intend to march us straight at the Nazis? I fancy we stay here until dark. They're bound to catch us in the daylight. I bet they radioed a description of us all over the place."

"You think so?" I smiled. "Just to catch a couple guys like us?"

Barney said in a sober voice, "That colonel will be bleedin' angry we escaped. And besides pricking his pride, it'll add to his ideas about us as spies. We better keep a watchful eye out. What do you make of this farmhouse?"

"I've been thinking about it. There are Germans, but also food. If we could swipe some food, I'd feel better about starting out again. It's gonna be a long walk, and we won't be able to hitchhike with German tanks and armored cars all over."

"Right. But we may have to walk for days. By that time, the information we have might not be much use. Archer, we've got to get back quick and not by walking the entire way."

"You got a better idea?" I said with a flash of anger in my voice.

Barney shrugged.

"Look," I said, "we'd be taking a heck of a chance by trying to thumb a ride. Maybe if we moved closer to that road over there, an empty truck or something might come by. We could slip aboard for a little ways and catch a ride."

We hiked down closer to the road. It was as if Lady Luck waited for us at that exact moment. In the sky to the east, I heard the throbbing drone of a German plane. We swiveled around and shielded our eyes with our hands, looking upward. The plane was down low and coming straight toward us. Panic gripped me. I grabbed Barney and we dove under the bushes.

I pointed after the plane. "Maybe they got planes out looking for us now. Don't move. Maybe they won't see us."

We stayed crouched under the protecting bush branches and squinted up at the plane. "It's a biplane with a swastika marking," Barney said. "I recognize it now. It's a two-seater Arado Ar 95. An old type torpedo plane. He cut his engine already and is gliding down. We need to get out of here. That observer in the back probably spotted us."

"Wait," I hissed and shot my hand out to stop Barney from leaping to his feet and dashing off into the woods. "If they've already spotted us, we won't get far before getting caught. I don't think they've seen us. Look, he's going into a gliding turn. I bet you a million bucks he's gonna land in that smooth field over there."

Barney nodded. "Some of those Germans in the farmhouse are running out to meet them. But what if they're telling them where we are?"

"They wouldn't land. They'd drop a message or use the radio if they had one. They'd stay in the air to see which way we headed. That's some kind of headquarters over there." I pointed at the farmhouse. "I bet that plane's bringing in a message."

"I hope you're right," Barney said in a shaky voice. His clear blue eyes clouded with doubt. "Look mate, he's on the ground, breaking to a stop."

"That is a sweet looking plane," I mumbled. "An Arado Ar 95, huh? I think I remember seeing pictures of that design. Has a BMW radial engine. I heard the Germans used them for training new pilots. Not as fast as the other planes, but I hear they're easy to fly." My hand was on Barney's arm, my fingers pinched into his skin.

"*Yow*. What's the matter with you, Archer? What's up?" Barney rubbed his arm.

I didn't answer. I watched the German plane come to a stop. The pilot and observer jumped down and jogged toward a group of Germans advancing from the farmhouse. They met and talked for a couple seconds. Then they all turned and went into the farmhouse. Once inside with the door closed, I took a quick look over at the Arado with its prop ticking over and then swung to face Barney.

"Our problem is solved," I said in a strained whisper. "That plane."

"Plane?" Barney echoed with a frown. He had the funniest, confused look on his face. "What about it? You don't mean—"

"Why not? I made my first solo flight on a better plane than that. I bet I can handle it. What do you say? Faster than hitchhiking?"

Barney gulped and looked undecided. I took his silence and pressed my point. "This is the best chance we could have. In that plane, we could get behind the Allied defenses in no time. Let's give it a shot. We could be stuck here for months and there's no telling what we could run into. What do you say? Are you game?"

My English pal was already smiling and nodding his head. "I'm game. Anything is better than sitting here waiting to get captured. We ought to make a good go of it."

I gave Barney a friendly punch to the shoulder. "I was hoping you'd say that." I felt energized and awake as a new adrenaline rush pulsed through me. "They're all inside the farmhouse. If we keep behind that field wall, we can get up close without being seen. Then, on my signal, run for that plane. We can make it—*we've got to.*"

9

THE GERMAN PLANE was thirty yards away at the extreme end of the field wall. The propeller idled, filling the air with a purring sound that sent blood surging through my veins in a wild excitement. Any fatigue or wariness in my body was gone. All I had left was a thrill of adventure surging through me with a renewed sense of strength peppered with a grim determination.

I rose onto one knee like a track runner at his mark on the starting line. I glanced over my shoulder at Barney and nodded.

"Now," I whispered. We took off like rabbits around the end of the field wall.

I reached the plane at least a dozen steps ahead of Barney and leaped into the cockpit. I snapped the safety belt buckle on while Barney scrambled into the observer's cockpit.

"I'm in," Barney shouted from behind.

I kicked off the wheel brake release. Then I grabbed hold of the control stick with my right hand. I reached for the throttle with my left and eased it forward. The BMW engine roared in a song of power and grace. I opened the throttle more and pushed the control stick ahead to get the tail up as our plane lumbered forward.

"Hurry Archer," Barney yelled above the roar of the engine. "They've seen us. They're running out of the house with bloody rifles."

A sharp bark of rifle fire terrified me as I hunched over the controls. A blood-chilling wind of nickel jacketed bullets streaked above my head. I ducked down lower and shoved the throttle wide open. The plane bounced over the ground on its wheels. The tail was up, and then gas fed to the engine causing the plane to leap forward like a high strung racehorse jumping a barrier.

This burst of speed flung me back in the seat. For an instant, my hands were torn from the control stick. My feet were yanked free from the rudder pedals. I swerved the plane clear of a sudden dip in the field's surface. Then I pulled the control stick back toward my stomach.

Seconds ticked by as the plane's wheels still clung to the ground. When they finally lifted clear and our Arado nosed up toward the gold-washed blue sky, exhaled air burst from my lungs like an exploding shell. I coughed and spit and shook the sweat from my face. I held our plane at the correct climbing angle. The engine in the nose sang such a sweet song of power that, for a moment, it was in tune with the wild song of joy in my heart. Our plane was easy to handle, responding instantly from a touch of the rudder pedals or the control stick.

As our plane climbed upward, I twisted around in my seat and looked at Barney. My English pal was staring down at the field we just left. I followed his gaze and saw thirty men in German military uniforms on the field—half of them firing at us with rifles. The others made angry gestures for our plane to return.

"You better believe we're not going back down there," I shouted over the roar of the engine. "We're not that crazy."

Barney swiveled his head to face me, his eyes dancing with

excitement. He grinned and then clasped both of his hands above his head and rested his head on his palms. I barely heard him say, "Well done, mate."

I nodded at my English pal and then twisted back around. The instruments were all in German, but I was familiar enough with the language to read them. My altimeter needle was quivering on the eighteen-hundred-meter mark, which would be about six thousand feet. We were high enough, and I leveled off our climb onto an even keel. I glanced down at the ground below to get my bearings. The first thing I saw was a small village off to the left. Another look and my heart leaped in my chest. I saw the hill and single main street where trucks, armored cars, and artillery passed by in a steady, endless stream. What town was this? A friendly town? Directly under us? I licked my lower lip and shivered with a surge of excitement.

We couldn't have traveled over eight or nine miles north during our run for freedom last night. Maybe we went around in circles for twice the number of miles, but not more than ten miles in the direction we wanted to go. Barney tapped me on the shoulder. He pointed at the village and mouthed the word "Allies." I got the gist of what he meant and nodded. I wiped a sheet of sweat from my forehead with the back of my free hand, then turned back around. I glanced at the sun and tried to decide which direction was due west. Something was wrong with the compass on the instrument panel. The needle just spun in circles.

I remembered a tip from a Great War flying ace about finding your direction when you were lost. In the morning, if you could see the sun, all you had to do was keep the sun on your tail, and you'd be flying west. I applied the rudder so that the sun was mostly on my tail and focused on the vast spread of ground ahead.

The entire western horizon was one massive cloud of dirty, grey smoke streaked with tongues of livid red, orange, and yellow flame. Almost like the whole of Belgium was on fire. Closer even was a long banked river that cut down across the countryside from the northwest to the southeast. I stared at it hard, thinking it was a weird looking river when Barney tapped me on the shoulder again.

"That's the Prince Albert Canal," he shouted above the roar of the engine. "It's like the Belgian Maginot Line. The Germans could never have crossed it yet. If we can get past it, Brussels won't be far off."

I pointed and yelled over my shoulder, "Down there to the left. Germans are swarming across it like ants. There has to be a million pontoon bridges thrown across that canal. Look at all those Stuka dive bombers."

Could this be true? Hitler's advancing forces had already smashed through the defenses? Forcing the Belgian army to retreat to the south side of the canal? German troops and Panzer divisions rushing across pontoon bridges attacking Belgians with hundreds of Stuka dive bombers. My heart felt like it was lodged in my throat. A terrible history was being written today. My soul was on fire with a blazing desire to do something, anything, for the cause of justice and civilization. Freedom of the entire world would soon be at stake here.

But I had another job to do first. I lifted my gaze and peered at the smoke and flame-filled sky ahead. Besides the smoke and fire, dozens of planes were streaking and darting in all directions. The air was full of them. Layer after layer of planes reaching from low down over the battleground right up to the sun. As far as I could tell, not a single one was an Allied plane. They were all German.

Barney pounded on my shoulder for the third time. "Faster Archer, a Messerschmitt behind us." His voice tinged with fright and alarm. "I think he's chasing us. What if he tries to shoot us down? What do we do?"

I looked over my shoulder at the sleek needle-shaped plane with its low monoplane wing. I shouted, "We gotta keep going.

Once we get to the other side of the canal, we'll be safe. We can land there."

I only said those words to cheer up Barney. My heart pounded with fear and dread. My palms were so sweaty they slipped off the control stick. I glanced over my shoulder. The other plane came upon us like an express train overtakes a slow freighter. It was a Messerschmitt 110. A moment later, I saw the gunner-observer in the rear pit shove back his bullet-proof glass cockpit hatch and stand up, waving at us with both arms. He was signaling for us to land at once. But I pretended I didn't see them. I ran the palm of my free hand hard against the already wide open throttle as though I could get more speed and outrun the Messerschmitt.

It was a futile attempt, and in only a few seconds, the Messerschmitt pulled up alongside us. I looked across the airspace that separated us. A lump bounced into my throat so fast it almost bumped up against my back teeth. The German observer was still sending signals for us to land. But not with his arms. Now he was using the machine gun fixed to the swivel mounting that circled the rim of his cockpit. He was pointing his gun at us and tilting it down toward the ground as he nodded his helmeted head.

I stared at the gun like I was in a trance, hypnotized. Blood pounded in my temples. My body was on fire one instant and icy cold the next. Death stared at me, and I could hardly force my brain to think. I knew I couldn't keep flying. I had to do something. This German would open fire and turn my plane into a blazing inferno. I'd rather die fighting than surrender and face the wrath of Colonel Snout. This Messerschmitt had no doubt been sent after us. Who knew? Maybe Colonel Snout had been the German I'd seen climb out of the observer's pit of this plane I was trying to fly behind Belgian lines. It would've been easy for the German to phone the nearest airfield and have a plane sent—

Tac-a-tac-a-tac-a-tac-a-tac-a-tac-a-tac

A tongue of flame surged from the muzzle of the machine gun in the Messerschmitt. A savage yammer smashed my ears. Wavy trails of tracer smoke cut across the nose of our plane. The roar of his gun snapped me into action. But we had no guns. Our plane was not armed. We were a courier plane meant to be used far beyond the lines on safe missions only.

We were at the mercy of this Messerschmitt flying wing to wing with us. Even though I wasn't trained in aerial combat, it was terrifying to not put up some kind of fight for our lives.

"It was a good try, mate," Barney called out. "But it's no use now. Nothing we can do but land."

The Messerschmitt fired a second warning burst that rattled and streaked across the front of our plane's nose. I reached out my hand to haul back the throttle. My hand froze in midair instead, and at that moment, I glanced at the ground below. What I saw steeled my nerves and gave me a fierce determination. We were over the Albert Canal. Belgian troops were digging in on the south side, wheeling guns into position, and throwing out rearguard action units. We were less than a half-mile from safety. This was too much. I thought of America's fighting spirit from Lexington and Concord, and it flamed up in my chest. I won't give up. I won't give in. I'll fight these Germans in the Messerschmitt. Let them try to shoot me down again. I didn't care if there were German planes all around. Maybe it was to my advantage. This Messerschmitt gunner would have to be careful to not hit any of his own planes.

Barney's voice was faint over the din of the engine roar. "Archer, he means it, turn back, or they'll shoot us down."

Barney's voice sounded like it came from a thousand miles away. I ignored it. I didn't even shake my head. My entire body was cold and numb with fear about what I was going to do. I had one thought. I steeled myself with only one determination. One purpose.

I eased back the throttle and let the nose drop. I applied

the stick and rudder like I was going to send the plane around and down in a gliding turn that would take us back east. As the plane turned, I shot a quick side glance at the Messerschmitt. My heart was ready to explode with joy. The German observer saw the movement of our plane and wrongly guessed its meaning. The man nodded his head and let go of his gun and sank back down into his seat.

At that instant, I thrust the throttle wide open again and shoved the stick forward until our plane was prop howling down in a vertical dive. "Hold on," I shouted at Barney without turning my head. "They don't have us yet, and they're not going to."

I braced myself against the speed of the dive and kept my mouth open so my eardrums wouldn't snap. I held myself hunched forward over the controls and fixed my eyes on the flames and smoke-smeared ground below us. The smoke and flames leaped up toward us at light speed. Out of the corner of my eye, I glimpsed Stuka dive bombers cutting through the air at a wicked speed. Then the deadly chatter of more German machine guns.

I didn't look back to see if that Messerschmitt was following me. I jammed hard on the left rudder and sent my plane swerving off to the side. The guns above me continued to yammer and snarl, but no bullets flew past my ears. I only heard the thunderous roar of our own BMW engine.

The Prince Albert Canal flashed by under my nose and was gone from view. I was across it and right over Belgian troops. We were roaring out of one danger zone and into another. I hadn't thought about the consequences of flying a plane with German markings over Belgian lines. When Belgian soldiers saw our swastika-painted plane streaking down at them, they would attack us with everything they had.

Maybe it was one of those freak things of war, or maybe Lady Luck was smiling on us again, but not a single Belgian bullet hit our diving plane. I hauled our plane out of its crazy, mad dive and streaked along to the rear of the Belgian lines. But before I traveled more than a couple miles, I heard one more snarl of aerial machine gunfire behind us. This time there was more to it than just the sound.

Our plane bucked and shuddered like it had been smashed by a fist of some invisible giant in the sky. Our plane's violent movement tore my hands from the controls and flung me over so hard I cracked my head on the cockpit and saw stars for a brief second. Then as soon as my senses cleared, I grabbed hold of the controls again. The engine and nose sputtered and coughed and shot out a cloud of thick black smoke—then died cold.

The first thing I did was yank back the throttle and cut off the ignition. Then I shoved the nose down and peered at the ground less than five-hundred feet below me. A groan of despair rose out of my throat and spilled off my lips. I didn't see a smooth patch of ground big enough for a fly to sit on. Plenty of fields, but they were pockmarked from one end to the other and full of shell and bomb craters. I glimpsed one spot where we could land without crashing too badly. But crash there we would. Nothing to do but try—

"We're gonna crash," I yelled over my shoulder. "Hold onto anything you can. Hang on tight."

10

I GLIDED our crippled plane down toward the bomb and shell marked field.

Fingers of fear gripped my heart. I'd made one or two forced landings in my short flying career, but it had been like setting down a plane on a gigantic pool table compared to what I had to do now. If I undershot that patch of ground, I'd plow into a battery of Belgian artillery guns hurling shells into hordes of onrushing Germans. And if I overshot that field or swerved too much, I'd crash into a maze of shell blasted tree stumps that would tear my plane to shreds.

I only had one hope now. And it was in hitting the center of that field and checking the forward roll of my plane. On impact, we would slide over and down into the bomb crater, and our crash wouldn't be too violent. I have one chance in a thousand of coming out of this mess without getting killed. Our fate was in the hands of the gods. Our plane's engine was dead—only one way to go now—down.

I jerked around and gave Barney one last look. He had said nothing for the last few minutes. Panic swept through me. Was Barney alright? Had he been hit? Is that why he wasn't talking? In the quick second it took to twist around and look, it felt like I had already died a hundred agonizing deaths.

Lady Luck was riding in the cockpit with both of us today. Barney was still alive. His lips were drawn back in a tight grin even though his face was ghostly white, and he had a glazed look in his eyes. As a pilot, Barney must know what this was all about. He had enough sense not to try any backseat flying. He left everything to me and trusted my judgment. He sat still in the seat and raised his arms, ready to throw them out across his face when we hit to protect himself.

Knowing that my pal was alright gave me new courage. I swiveled to the front. The ground was just under our wheels. I wasn't going to undershoot or overshoot that field. I'd proven my flying skills so far. Ten feet, nine feet, eight . . . seven . . . six . . . I jerked the control stick all the way back against my stomach. The nose rose a few inches and then the plane stalled and dropped. My body froze at the moment the plane stalled. I let go of the stick. I buried my head in my arms and let my whole body go limp.

Two seconds ticked by like two long years. Our plane hung motionless in the air. Then dropped belly first like a stone. The wheels hit hard. We bounced back into the air, hit hard on the ground, bounced again, and hit one more time. I felt the tail wheel catch on something and we plunged off to the right. I jammed the left rudder hard to counteract the movement, but it was too late. Fate placed a massive bomb crater in our way. Our plane slithered over the lip of the crater and we dove deep into an abyss.

It reminded me of a wild ride on a Coney Island roller coaster. Our plane twisted, wrenched, and lurched until landing on its side, halfway up the nose. We swayed there with the plane's tail pointing up at the sky. We'd rolled around twice like a revolver's gun barrel and then fell over with a thud. It felt like someone smacked me in the chest with a sledgehammer. The air in my lungs whistled out through my mouth. Colored lights whirled around my brain. The universe felt like it was filled with a rumble of roaring thunder.

Long seconds passed, my breath returned, the spinning stopped. I hung headfirst on my safety harness. I thought about Barney. I tried to twist around and look back. I couldn't move.

"Barney," I yelled in a choked voice. "Barney? Are you okay?" Nothing. A chilling silence answered my question and froze my heart.

Then a faint voice, "I'm alright Archer. But this blasted safety harness broke. And I'm down in a bloody puddle of mud. Can you give me a hand?"

I laughed hysterically. I tore at my safety belt buckles. I got them unfastened as quick as I could and grabbed hold of the sides of the cockpit before I tumbled into the muddy bottom of the bomb crater. I cartwheeled by accident and landed feet first. I got a look at Barney. Plonked down on the seat of his pants in eight inches of mud. Covered in mud from the top of his head all the way down. He'd landed square on his head but squirmed around and sat up before he suffocated. He was pawing the cakey mud off his face like windshield wipers with no wiper blades in a hurricane.

I plowed through the mud and lifted him up from under his armpits and heaved. Barney's body popped out of the mud like a chef tugging a cork from a bottle of wine. I hung onto him and ducked under a section of the crumpled wing. I yanked and tugged and heaved us out of the crater to plop on firm, dry ground. I dug out a handkerchief from my pocket and handed it to my English pal.

I held up a V with my fingers.

Barney snorted and squinted out of one of his mud-caked eyes. "Next time, I'm flying the bloody plane."

"That was an awful landing," I said. "Maybe I thought I was too good. Next time I'll let you do the flying."

"Rotten landing? They can't fly any better than that in the

RAF. I thought for sure we were both going to get killed. Neither of us have a scratch."

"It was luck. I was scared stiff. Good thing those Messerschmitt guys were a bunch—"

A squad of Belgian infantry raced across the field toward us. Their bayonets glistened in the sun on the ends of their rifles. Screams and wild cries burst from their lips. *Wait.* These Belgians think we're Nazis. They're racing over here to kill us. To get vengeance for what the Stuka dive bombers have done to them. I pushed myself up and waved my hands over my head. One of the running soldiers tossed his rifle up to his shoulder and fired. The bullet cut past my face so close I felt the heat and heard the hiss. I leaped in front of Barney, still wiping his face, and flung both of my palms forward.

"Wait. Don't shoot, don't shoot," I yelled in French. "We're not Germans. America. England. Don't shoot. *Vive les Alliés.*"

The Belgian soldiers rushed up to us and leveled their rifles at our stomachs. Their eyes were bloodshot, their faces caked with dried mud. Their uniforms were torn, and some even ripped to rags from the fury of the war hurled down on them for the last seventy-two hours. The only clean thing about them was their rifles.

A soldier with a corporal's chevrons on his tattered sleeve stepped forward. The tip of his bayonet balanced on the Adam's apple of my throat. "You are *les Boches,*" he said in French and pointed at the wrecked plane. "We watched you dive on us. You will not dive again. We—"

"Wait, wait," I shouted in a butchered French. "We not German. He's English and I'm American. We escaped Germany. We prisoners there. We get to Allied headquarters at once. We have information. Valuable information."

The Belgian corporal hesitated and looked puzzled. It was obvious his men didn't believe me. They had scowling frowns and made snarling sounds in their throats, slowly stepping closer. I opened my mouth to explain more. Barney pulled me back from the bayonet and stepped forward. A stream of clear French words poured from his thin, muddy lips.

"Listen to me, you *dutskes*," he shouted in clear French and pointed at them. "*Mon amie* tells the truth. We've just escaped from Germany and have important information. Do we look like Germans? Where are your brains? Have you not seen us risk our lives trying to reach this side of the lines? Take us to your commanding officer at once. He may even recommend you for a metal. Do you hear me? I will make a personal complaint to the commander-in-chief of the British Army, General Gort. Take us to your commanding officer now!"

The corporal chuckled and lowered his bayonet. The battle weary Belgian soldiers grinned. "The little one spits fire when he speaks," the Belgian corporal said in English. "I don't believe now that you're German. But you had a lucky escape. Follow me. I'll take you to my lieutenant." The Belgian corporal shrugged and wiped his tired eyes with his mud and dirt-smeared hand.

We trudged along next to the Belgian soldiers, avoiding crater holes and dead soldiers littering the torn-up earth. "Can you hold the Germans back?" Barney asked. "Aren't the British and the French helping you?"

"I don't know," the Belgian corporal said. "It's possible, there are no British or French here. Only Belgians. And we can't stop these Germans. We don't have the guns, men, or tanks. We have no planes. All our planes are gone." He pointed up to the sky. "Filled with nothing but Boche planes. It's bad for us, but we're not afraid to die."

The Belgian corporal shrugged and continued across the field, lugging his rifle like it weighed as much as a tank instead of the few pounds it did. Barney and I dropped into step with the others. No one spoke. We only heard the sounds of the bombs and shells a few miles away, quickly coming closer.

I leaned toward Barney. "I don't blame them. They

must've been through something wicked here. We're lucky they didn't shoot us and ask questions after we were already killed."

Barney smiled. "If you kept trying to speak French to them, they'd probably have shot you."

"Yea," I said. "You can blabber better than me. But you're still short and English."

Barney scrunched his lips and shook his head.

I yawned. A wave of exhaustion washed over me. I felt old. Like my strength had been sapped to the limit, and my spirits were staggering under a heavy crushing weight. I closed my eyes and pictured the German hordes pouring across the Albert Canal. Crushing the Belgians like a mighty tidal wave, crashing forward with nothing but a picket fence to stop it.

We trailed the Belgians and turned left onto a winding, narrow dirt road. We went down this path for another fifty yards and then entered the woods. In the heart of the woods were several companies of Belgian troops. They moved frantically, building up their machine-gun emplacements and uncoiling barbed wire. They dragged artillery field pieces into place to bear on the winding dirt road. The corporal stopped in front of a young lieutenant and saluted. We stopped and waited while the corporal spoke to the officer.

A couple moments later, the lieutenant came over and stared at us with bleak, dead tired eyes. "What's all this about?" He said in a flat voice.

I nodded to Barney. After living on the continent for a few years, he spoke French like a native. Barney blabbed about our story for several minutes. He recounted our movements since the Nazi armies broke into Belgium until we crashed the plane in the field. The Belgian officer listened in silence. When Barney finished, the lieutenant took a map from his pocket and spread it out on the ground.

"Where were some of those pins and flags on that map?" the lieutenant asked.

Barney did the talking. I watched while he pointed out various points on the map. The Belgian lieutenant nodded his head from time to time and then folded the map and got to his feet. "I'm positive you've seen an important map. I'll get you to Belgian GHQ at once. You must tell them all you know. They'll communicate with the Allied high command. You've done a good thing here."

Barney's face flushed, and he looked uncomfortable. "We just want to help."

"If I only had a million more like you under my command," the lieutenant said. His tired lips twisted back into a wistful smile as he glanced from me to Barney. "If only half of what you say is true, it's more than enough. Sergeant."

A bearded Belgian sergeant putting a machine gun in working order got to his feet and lumbered over. He ran his bloodshot eyes over Barney and me, then fixed them on the officer.

"These two," the lieutenant said, jerking his head toward us. "Take them to General Michiels. Take one of the light scouting cars and drive them there at once."

The massive sergeant blinked and had a puzzled look on his face. "I'll try my lieutenant. But we may run into difficulty. A runner arrived a moment ago. Boche tanks cut off the road to Namur. They're trying to get behind us. Boche planes are bombing the whole road. It will be difficult, but I'll try."

The Belgian lieutenant's face paled under a coating of blood and dirt. He clenched his fists in a helpless gesture, and something close to tears of bitter rage glistened in his haggard eyes. At that moment, the universe felt like it was filled with an eerie scream. Belgians dove to the ground and fell flat on their faces. The lieutenant shoved me to the ground and tried to cover me with his body.

I knew that sound. I'd heard it along that road—that road packed with the tears of the terror-stricken refugees. I remember dragging that old woman to the filthy protection of an ox cart. My heart stood upright in my chest. Blood ceased to surge through my veins. My lungs locked with air, and my brain became numb and useless as I waited through these terrible seconds.

The diving Stukas death load hit on the far side of the road. Half of Belgium seemed to fountain up into the sky. What was left rocked and swayed. A thunderous sound swept over me and pushed me further down to the ground. In a crazy sort of way, I wondered if I was dead. Then the Belgian lieutenant pulled me to my feet.

"It's only the direct hits that matter," the Belgian officer said in a gentle voice.

"Direct enough for me," I said.

"When they dive, several at a time, it's not pleasant," the Belgian officer said. "But there's nothing you can do. That's the way with war. About this trip to General Michiels' headquarters. You heard what the sergeant said. Could be dangerous. You want to wait here and rest first?"

I jerked my head up. "Ready to start right now. Okay, Barney?"

Barney nodded. "Right then. Let's go, mate."

"Very well," the Belgian officer said. "Perhaps it's not best to wait here. We will soon be very busy. Sergeant! You have your orders."

The tired Belgian officer clicked his heels and saluted us. We returned his salute. I looked into his eyes and saw a look I would never forget. That Belgian officer knew what he was in for. He knew he'd have to stay where he was and face it. I'm sure he also knew he'd never live to see another sunrise. His loyalty and courage stirred me to the depth of my soul. I reached out and grabbed the officer's hand to shake it.

"I hope you can beat them back lieutenant," I said in a rush of words. "We'll be rooting for you." I tried to blink away the tear forming in my eye.

Barney chimed in. "I bloody well hope you chase them all the way back to Berlin."

The lieutenant smiled at us and saluted again. We turned away and followed the massive, bearded sergeant to the patch of woods to the far side, where a unit of scouting tanks and small cars were parked under the trees. The sergeant got behind the wheel of the nearest scouting car and motioned us to get in back. A couple of moments later, the engine was doing its work. Sergeant Big Beard skillfully drove the car across the open fields toward the southwest.

Belgian troops were in a frenzy of activity all around us. I realized the Belgians were making feverish preparations for a last-ditch stand against the Germans. The nightmare of the Albert Canal crossing was still fresh in my mind. In my heart, I knew this was only a gallant effort. Those German hordes, protected by the swarms of planes, would cut right through the Belgians. My chest felt hollow yet heavy as I watched them toil in what I knew in my heart would be vain. I slumped down in the back seat. I let my body sway with the bumps and stared at the back of our driver's neck.

"Cheer up, Archer," Barney said. "We'll get through this alright. You just wait and see."

"I'm not worried about that. I was just thinking."

"About what?"

"About these poor Belgians and that plane I cracked up. I feel terrible about that. I wish I could've brought it down in one piece."

"You were lucky to get it down in mostly one piece. If it was me, I would've killed us both for sure."

"Still want to fly the next plane we steal?" I said, trying to force back the sarcasm.

"Now I can tell you I didn't believe you could fly and was bloody scared when we took off. But it looks like you proved me wrong. You're a little bit of alright, Archer. I really mean that."

"Stop being such a sap. Aren't you supposed to be English?"

"That's as syrupy as I get, mate. And the last bloody compliment I ever give you."

"Ah, come on, pal. Don't be that way."

Barney shook his head, folded his arms across his chest and raised his eyebrows.

"Alright, alright," I said. "Let me tell you something, I made a nasty landing on my first solo. I cracked up the plane. I busted a wing and wiped out the undercarriage. I didn't get a scratch. I was so scared I busted out of that plane crying like some kid. My instructor thought something horrible happened to me. But when I finally got it out, he was okay with the whole thing. He said it was a normal reaction for someone who could really go for flying. It made me feel better, anyway."

"So, what's your point, Archer? That this isn't the first plane you've wrecked and—"

Barney's eyes widened like tractor tires, and he gasped. Our car bounced out of the field and swung onto a road blossomed with geysers of brilliant red flame and towering columns of oily black smoke. A thunderous sound rushed at us. Our small scouting car jerked to a halt.

"Shrapnel barrage," the sergeant screamed. "Take cover under the car."

11

ALL THREE OF us cowered under the car while the German gunners fired a fury of screaming steel and mountains of flame.

I jammed my palms to my ears while the whole world around me went mad with shot and shell. Never in my life have I heard such a roaring, crashing sound. My body was paralyzed with fear. But when I didn't die—I felt numb. The rumbling thunder had no more of an effect on me. Was it courage coming to my rescue? Because it wasn't from a lack of fear. In the middle of that furious bombardment, I was too stunned to register any emotion.

It only lasted ten minutes. The range of the guns changed, and the barrage moved onward to another objective. None of us moved. It was like each of us waited for the other to make the first move. I couldn't stand the suspense. I poked my head up without thinking and cracked it hard on the underside of the car. I yelped like I'd been stung by a bee. The sound of my voice seemed to release whatever was holding Barney and Sergeant Big Beard back.

We crawled out from under the car, got to our feet, and looked around. Sergeant Big Beard shrugged and muttered through his teeth. There wasn't any more road. It was completely gone. Lost in a vast area of smoking shell holes that stretched out in all directions as far as the eye could see. Blackened jagged stumps marked what once were trees. Fields that were once green, spring grass transformed into brown acres full of dirt and stones. That spot where I'd last seen a farmhouse was now as bare as the palm of my hand.

"You two are a lucky charm," Sergeant Big Beard said, bobbing his head up and down, looking us over. "You can stay by my side always. Perhaps, I might just come out of this war alive. Look at our car. Just a cracked window and a dent."

Our small scouting car was bathed in dirt and dust. Broken glass littered the ground. One of the passenger-side windows was shattered and a tree trunk projectile smashed in the hood. But the engine idled as smooth as could be. Sergeant Big Beard stared at it like he was lost in a dream. Then he shook his head and muttered through his buck teeth and climbed in behind the wheel.

The sergeant zipped our car in and around the bomb craters with careless ease. He skirted around a patch of woods toward a yet untouched road. And to make this trip even more unbearable, he began singing in off-key French at the top of his lungs.

For the next half hour, the war faded away even though there were signs of it on all sides and above our heads. A certain feeling of security washed over me as Sergeant Big Beard bumped along the road, dodging shell holes, artillery batteries, and reserve troops being rushed up to the front. A few hours ago, I had been hiding in enemy territory. Barney and I were hunted prisoners of war. But now, we were well behind the Belgian lines, speeding toward a headquarters where we would deliver our information about enemy positions of great value to the Allies. Barney and I, both only seventeen, had beaten the Germans at their own game.

Instead of revealing information to the Germans—we'd escaped with German information valuable to the Allies.

I leaned my head back. It felt good to know that I'll have been at least some help in this war. It made me feel better to know that I had a friend like Barney James with me. Barney proved himself in my eyes. And even though he was being modest, Barney probably would've done a better job of flying that plane. At every turn, my English pal popped up with a new side to him. I was lucky and glad that I stumbled into Barney and his ambulance, and that they came along when they did. How long had it been now? Three days or three years? I can't even keep track of the time anymore.

Barney sat up and tapped the Belgian sergeant on the shoulder. "Why are you heading east?" He pointed at the last rays of the setting sun. "If you're trying to get to Namur, you're going the wrong way."

"You're right," the sergeant called over his shoulder. "Les Boches have cut the road. We must go around them. It will be dark soon. It won't be hard when it's dark. Don't worry, we'll get there."

Barney looked at me and rolled his eyes. He sat upright in his seat like he wanted to argue, but then looked like he thought better of it. He slowly sank back into his seat with a scowl on his face and just stared at the setting sun.

"What gives," I asked. "You don't think Sergeant Big Beard knows what he's doing?"

Barney smirked and mouthed the words *Big Beard?*

"No, he's right." Barney leaned in closer. "If the Namur road was cut up by the Germans, we've got a go around. It's just . . . I spent several summers in this part of Belgium and—"

Barney leaned forward again. "Sergeant, why can't we circle around them to the west? We can cut over and take the road leading south from Wavre."

Sergeant Big Beard jammed on the brakes so suddenly, I almost launched over the back of the front seat.

"*Mon Dieu!*" he shouted and thumped his enormous fist against his forehead. "Of course, of course. The bombs and shells. They must've made scrambled eggs out of what I have in my head."

The sergeant shifted back into low gear and got back underway again. At a crossroads, one hundred yards ahead, he turned sharp right and stomped on the gas. A moment later, a machine gun rumbled behind us. I twisted around and saw an armored car with the German swastika racing for the turnoff we'd taken, but from the opposite direction. A machine gun was mounted in the vehicle, and a helmeted German soldier was determined to get us in range.

Sergeant Big Beard glanced over his shoulder and stomped on the gas. "Again, what a lucky charm you are." He shouted and hunched forward over the wheel. "If you hadn't put sense in my head and I turned off onto this road, we'd have run right into the Germans."

Barney and I looked at each other and didn't say a word. I was too busy hanging on to whatever life I had left and trying to stay in the car as it rocketed forward—leaping across shell holes in the road. Sergeant Big Beard wasn't the brightest pebble on the beach, but he knew how to handle our car. He skipped across the shell holes, dodged and twisted around trees that were blown down, and roared through the scattered wreckage of bombed-out supply trucks while the machine gun behind us snarled and yammered its death song.

The pursuing Germans swung out onto the road and struggled to overtake us. I stuck my head up to see if they'd gained any ground, but before my head popped out of its turtle shell, Barney grabbed me by the waist and hurled me down on the floor of the car.

"Stay down, Archer! Are you mad?" he shouted above the

roar of the scouting car's powerful engine. "We've dodged enough bullets for one day."

I gave Barney a sheepish grin and nodded. "That was dumb. Thanks."

A burst of bullets whined low over the car. I gulped and ducked my head even lower. Our little car spun to the right and caught air. We came down with a crashing jolt. A shower of bush branches slithered down on us. We were tossed around in the back of the car like a pair of dice in a cup. I was puffing and panting and struggled to brace myself before I was pitched out head over heels onto the cratered shell road. No sooner would I get a hold on something in the car before Sergeant Big Beard would dart off in another direction, and I'd get bounced around like a hot potato all over again.

For another ten minutes, we tore through the darkening twilight, first this way, then that. Then the jolting stopped. The car ran on an even keel. I felt bumps and bruises biting my body from head to toe. I scrambled up off the floor of the car and flopped back down on the seat. Sergeant Big Beard stopped our car under a shelter of overhanging tree branches. He switched the engine off and turned around and smiled at us. He had a goofy but triumphant look on his face.

"We have lost les Boches," he said. "Everything is alright. When it gets dark, we will continue. Merci, my lucky charms."

"A fine bit of driving," Barney said, "but you came too bloody close to breaking my neck."

Sergeant Big Beard boomed a hardy laugh and gestured with his big hands. "That was nothing. These little cars can go up the side of a cliff. That German thing? It drives like a snail. Should have been with the lieutenant and me yesterday. That was a wild ride. They shot at us from all sides for an hour. Even so, we got through without a scratch."

"I'm glad I wasn't there," Barney said. "But now what? Where are we?"

The Belgian stuffed a dirty cigarette between his lips and

lit up. "Now we wait for darkness, not much longer. He pointed across the field to the left. "One or two miles in that direction and we'll find the road to Namur. From there, it's three hours at the most."

"Unless the Germans bombed that road too," I said.

Sergeant Big Beard looked at me and snorted. "Impossible, no way they could have advanced that far. Don't worry, I will get you to Namur in no time. I—"

A thumping of gunfire broke out from behind us and to the left—a deep booming sound of long-range pieces, but also a sharp bark of small caliber guns. Sergeant Big Beard pinched out his cigarette and slid out of the car. He stood still for a moment, cocked his head to one side and listened closely toward the direction of the guns. I couldn't tell if they were coming closer. It was impossible to tell because the nearby strip of woods broke up the sound.

I noticed the worried look on the Belgian sergeant's face. He had deep lines that signaled he was trying to convince himself that the truth was false. In the fast-fading lights, his face deepened until it became a mask of shadows. Then he muttered something under his breath and pulled his pistol from his hip holster.

"Stay here," the sergeant said in a firm voice. "This is strange. I have to investigate. I'm getting a quick look and then I'll return."

Sergeant Big Beard slipped away from the car and was swallowed up by the shadows cast from the trees. I looked at Barney. "What do you think? If those are Germans coming this way, we'd be crazy to stay here."

"Maybe, but they might not be. Let's give it a little bit here. Wouldn't be too fair driving off and leaving the sergeant to walk back."

"That was a wild ride. Good thing you told him what you did when you did. He saved us from another tough spot."

Machine gunfire echoed through the woods. Barney

jumped out of the car and waved at me. "We better look, Archer," he said in a worried voice. "If the Germans are close, we have no chance in that car. Our best bet is to hide out in the woods until they pass."

I jumped out of the car and grabbed Barney by the arm. "You think . . . You think the sergeant bumped into them and got killed?"

"I think so, mate," he said with a concerned look on his face. "We better go make sure, though."

"Sure," I said, although I didn't feel so on the inside. "Lead on. Right behind you."

12

We crept forward through the woods. Toward the spot where we heard the sharp burst of machine-gun fire. Before we made it one-hundred yards in, I heard a shout, stopping us in our tracks. From my high school German class, I could translate what he said to:

Just a Belgian dog. Probably a deserter. Good thing we shot him.

An icy cold gripped my chest. That bitter resentment toward the Nazis flamed up in me again. Barney crept forward on all fours and then flattened to the ground. We came to a break in the trees that gave us a view of a large field in the distance. Three German light tanks were parked in the field. A helmeted man, an officer, stood up in the gun turret of each tank. Sixty yards in front of the tanks, German soldiers bent over a crumpled figure on the ground. It was too dark to get a good view. But I didn't need a clear view. Sergeant Big Beard was dead. He would never drive or fight or laugh or sing again.

"Bloody animals," Barney whispered. "Three tanks against one Belgian sergeant. He was a good bloke. To hell with these Germans."

"If I had a machine gun right now," I whispered—anger

seeping from my voice. "I wish. I wish I had a machine gun right now."

"Not against tanks, Archer. We'd be cooked. We've got to go at it alone again. Now, if they would just . . ."

Barney didn't have to finish the sentence. I had the same thought. If those tanks turned off to the right, our car wouldn't be discovered. We could still try to make Namur. But if the tanks turned left, toward the woods where we crouched. They'd spot our car and blow it to bits with their armor-piercing guns if they didn't take it for themselves.

My heart raced, and I had an urge to pee. I held my breath while the tank engines clanked to life. When they inched forward, I wanted to yell with relief. The farthest tank from us wheeled around on its treads to the right. The second tank followed. And then the third. They made a racket that echoed and boomed back and forth through the war swept countryside. The tanks moved out of the field and rumbled down over the lip of the slope and were soon lost to view. I let the air out of my lungs and whistled.

"A break at last," I said. "We can use that scouting car now."

"You're bloody right we can." Barney leaped to his feet. "It's a Renault too. I'm driving."

"Then you're the chauffeur," I said. "Let's go."

We were back in our scouting car in less than a minute, and Barney kicked the engine into life. He shifted into gear, and we continued in the direction our sergeant had shown us before he was killed in the woods.

"I hope he knew what he was talking about," Barney yelled above the sound of the gears grinding. "After that crazy ride, I'm not sure where we are. But I'll recognize the road to Namur when we get to it. It's one of the few decent roads in Belgium." Barney stomped on the gas. My head snapped back, and I clutched for anything to hold on to.

Riding in the front seat of our scouting car was much

better—easier on my bones, bumps, and bruises. Even though the car raced along across a rough, uneven surface, I didn't get half of the bouncing around while sitting up front. But when we rushed up to a group of trees, Barney yanked down on the wheel and swerved past with a couple feet to spare. I pressed my elbows into my sides and tried to make my body as small as possible.

"It's fun driving these," Barney shouted. "A Renault is a good car. My father has one."

I shouted back, "How about some lights? It's getting dark."

Barney nodded and flicked up a switch on the dashboard.

Two pale beams of light swept out in front of our car. They helped some but were too dim and did not put me at ease. Dark objects whipped into view and then slipped by as Barney wrenched the wheel this way or that. We bounced out of a field onto a dirt road. We were tearing along the road heading west.

Barney slammed on the brakes, swung to the side of the road, and switched off the lights. "Planes, hear 'em? Might've seen our lights. They're German and flying low too."

A throbbing, pulsating hell of thunder rolled toward us out of the sky. The planes were a couple thousand feet up, and from the sound, at least a couple squadrons. We squinted up and saw an armada of wings sweeping forward against the stars. Their lights were off. Their position was given away by the bluish glow of the engine exhaust plumes trailing backward.

"At least a hundred of them," I said. "They look like Heinkels. I wonder where they're headed. Look at them Barney, isn't that something?"

Barney was silent. He peered up at the death armada as it went by and his mouth fell open slightly. "They're headed for the same place we are. Namur. I'm sure of it."

"So what?" I said.

Barney inhaled a long breath. "I bet five pounds the Germans know Belgian HQ is at Namur, and they're going to take it out. Is that clear enough for you?"

"No need to be so grumpy," I said. "All we can do now is keep going."

The roar of the bombers faded away to the south. Barney started the car and switched on the lights. Five minutes later we came to a well-paved broad highway.

"That poor Belgian sergeant was right," Barney shouted and turned south on the road.

"Look." I pointed ahead. "That red glow way down there. It's like the horizon is on fire. Wait. Do you hear that? Hear the sounds? I bet those are planes dropping bombs."

Barney sped up the car. "Blimey! We're too late. I bet Belgian HQ cleared out of here long ago. We'll never find them there if that's even Namur." Barney pounded on the top of the steering wheel with a clenched fist.

For the next few minutes, neither of us spoke. We gawked at the ever-increasing red glow mounting higher into the horizon sky. A red glow mixed with streaks of yellow and flashes of vivid orange. The *Pahrump Pahrump Pahrump* of high explosive bombs detonating vibrated our car. It reminded me of a movie I'd seen about the world coming to an end—the apocalypse. The scenic effects had been like what we watched now. Only it hadn't been half as vivid or as heart chilling as this. But that was a movie. This is a real war. Way off there in the distance, the city was dying. Bombs from war-making maniacs were smashing a living city into a powdery ruin. What a horrible nightmare. What can I do? What should I do?

Barney tugged at my shoulder, forcing me to tear my eyes from the terrifying spectacle. I jerked my arm away. "What? What is it?"

He pointed down the highway. "Lights coming. Got a strange feeling about this, Archer."

The highway had been empty ever since we got onto it. "Yep. This can't be good. That's not a car. The lights aren't together."

"What if they're German? We better hop out and—"

"Too late now," I said. The lights swerved toward our side of the road. "They've seen us. Here they come."

A pair of motorcycles roared up beside our car. Their brakes shrieked to a halt. Two shadowy figures vaulted from their saddles. A white flashlight beam pointed straight into my face and blinded me. I froze and felt like my legs were tree branches—rooted to the spot. I wanted to shout we weren't soldiers, but the words wouldn't come out.

A voice in French called out, "Who are you? What is this? *Nom de Dieu!* Two boys and a scouting car?"

I dropped to my knees in an unexpected release of tension. Tears welled up behind my eyelids.

Barney answered in French. "We're trying to reach General Michiels' headquarters. We have important information. Take the bloody light out of my bleedin' eyes already, will you? We're not armed."

The soldier lowered his bright light. It took several seconds before I could adjust my eyes back to the pitch darkness. After blinking four hundred times, I realized two Belgian corporals stood in front of us. Their eyes were narrowed, almost squinting, and their pistols were drawn—ready to shoot us.

"General Michiels?" one of them said. "Why do you want to see him? What are you doing in this scouting car? Did you steal it? Are you going to take it to your family and fill it with furniture?"

"Nuts!" I yelled at them in English. "We're not Belgian. He's English and I'm an American. We've escaped from Germany with valuable information. A Belgian lieutenant gave us this car and a sergeant to drive it. He's back there in the woods, dead. We bumped into three German tanks and—"

"German tanks?" one of the corporals replied in English. "Where?"

"Back there," I said, and pointed in the general direction where we had come from. "Is General Michiels still in Namur?"

The Belgian corporals looked at each other. Their faces were painted with a grimace. One corporal spoke in fast French, "If they saw Boche tanks, must be a flanking movement to cut us off from Brussels. We must move at once."

His partner nodded and turned to head back to his motorcycle.

"Wait," I shouted. "Is General Michiels in Namur or what?"

"Nothing in Namur except death and dying. It's full of Germans," the corporal said, pressing his fist to his mouth. "We're going to the general's new headquarters. You can follow us. But hurry, unless you want to get shot or taken prisoner. Those tanks you saw mean we are surrounded by those butchers."

The Belgian corporals vaulted onto their saddles and opened their motorcycle engines with a roar that bounced clear up to the stars. They were off like bullets and over one-hundred yards ahead of us before Barney could turn our car around. Once we were pointed in the right direction, we didn't waste any time. We chased behind the two motorcycles like we were in a wind tunnel. I clung to the side of the car and blew out a series of quick breaths while Barney drove us into hell.

The Belgians roared another mile up the road, then swerved off to the left onto a road that led northwest.

"They're heading for Brussels," Barney shouted as the wind howled past the car. "The sergeant was right when he said it looks bad. The Germans must be deep into the country—"

"Barney, watch out," I shouted and pointed ahead.

The road ahead burst open into a sea of blinding light and collapsing earth. The two Belgian corporals melted into it and disappeared. It was like invisible hands snatched our small car and tossed it into the air. From a million miles away, I heard Barney screaming my name. I felt like I was spinning end over end through a white-hot fire of billowing black smoke. A million wild, crazy thoughts whirled around in my brain, and then everything turned black.

13

A KIND FACE. The smile was friendly and warm. But I couldn't keep it in focus. It was so close to me for one moment and seemed so real. Then a cloud would pass in front, and the face would fade away. I tried to focus on that face. The mouth was talking to me, but I couldn't hear a word.

Everything was so calm and quiet. Everything was white. Except that kind-looking face. I stared at it hard. I tried to force it into focus. But my eyes were so heavy. I was so sleepy. Why couldn't I stop seeing that face? Was I sleeping?

Maybe this was a dream, and I was asleep. But why was I sleeping? I shouldn't be sleeping. What was the last thing I did? What was the last thing I saw? Barney and I were following motorcycles toward General Michiels' headquarters. But something happened. What was it? I know I didn't fall asleep while Barney was driving. Of course not. Wait, more was coming back to me. An explosion. An explosion on the road ahead, and the two Belgian soldiers disappeared into it. Where am I? Why is everything white? Why is that kind-looking face fading in and out in front of me? Why can't I hear those words that the moving lips are saying? Am I dead? Is this what it's like when you die? Barney. Where is Barney

James? I couldn't find any answers. My head ached so much I just kept looking at that face that made me sleepy—so sleepy.

And then the face stopped fading away into the depths of a foggy mist. It stayed right there, right where I was. When the lips moved, I heard, "How do you feel? Does your head hurt much?"

My head? Why are those lips asking me if my head hurts? My head didn't hurt at all. Nothing about me hurt. I felt fine. I'm okay. What's going on? Wait. I'm in a bed under sheets and blankets. I pushed myself up onto my left elbow and looked around. I'm in a hospital. A long line of beds down each side of a vast room painted so white it hurts my eyes. There was a man—a soldier—in every bed. Uniforms hung on hooks on the wall. There was that face again. That face was a captain in the British Army, in the Medical Corps. I recognized the insignia on his lapels.

"Steady, lad," The officer said in a soothing voice. "Tell me now, how's the head feel? How's the pain?"

I blinked. I opened my mouth to speak but couldn't utter a word at first. My mouth was dry. "My head's okay, sir," I muttered. "I feel fine. Where am I? What's going on? We're in the hospital?"

The medical officer let out a sigh like he was holding his breath for a long time. "Splendid," he said. "You're out of it at last. You might be alright now. But you had a close one. You might've remained in a coma for weeks or months. That concussion shock is no joke. Want something to eat?"

"Sure," I said. "Okay, wait. I remember now. Where's my pal? Where's Barney James? He was with me when that road exploded."

"Road exploded?" the medical officer said and raised his eyebrow. "I think you mean it was a landmine. Your pal's name is Barney James? English soldier?"

"He's not a soldier yet. But he's a volunteer. Where is he? Please tell me he's not killed? I gotta know if he's . . . ?"

The officer leaned down and patted me on the shoulder. "Your pal's alright," he said and pointed to Barney asleep in the next bed. "He came out of it for the last time a few hours ago. He raved about crazy things, so I gave him something to sleep. He'll be fine when he wakes up. Now, tell me about this landmine—or the road exploding, as you say?"

"I don't exactly know," I said. "Barney was driving our Belgian scouting car, and we were following a couple of motorcycle riders to find General Michiels. We turned off toward the Namur road. And then *bam*. Everything went dark. How did we get here? Did someone scoop us up off the road?" I tilted my head. "Did I say something funny?"

The officer wiped a broad smile from his lips.

"I'm not laughing at you," he said. "The effects of concussion shock should be no joke. You've been in a military hospital here at Lille for eight days."

My throat tightened and my eyes widened. I felt a blank amusement. Did I hear that right? My ears must be playing tricks on me. Eight days?

The medical officer leaned in like he was reading my thoughts. "It's been exactly eight days this morning since they brought you two here."

"But eight days?" I said. "I'm not even that hurt. I've got no bandages, and I'm not in any pain. How could I have been here for eight days?"

"I'll spare you the medical explanation because you probably wouldn't understand," the medical officer said, raising his eyebrows and giving me a glassy stare. "What happened was something like this. The concussion shock of that explosion, whatever it was, temporarily paralyzed certain nerve centers in your body and in your head. Why you didn't receive any physical injury is just one of those mysterious things that happen in war." The medical officer reached for the pencil in the chart. "A shell can blow every strip of clothing off a soldier's back, blow his shoes off, and toss him fifty yards but still not leave him with a single scratch. That's what must've happened to you and your pal. Maybe, being in the scouting car, you were protected from those things flying around. But certain nerve centers were paralyzed. There is little we can do for that outside of a few injections. You probably don't remember waking up several times? Do you?"

I shook my head. "No, sir. But I remember seeing a face that kept fading in and out and seeing lips move, but I couldn't hear words."

The medical officer nodded. "That's usually the way it works. It's just your nerve system returning to normal. You could see a little, but you couldn't hear. Or you could feel but not have the power to speak. The medical term for it has thirty-six letters. I'll have the nurse bring you something to eat."

"Wait," I said. "Have I gone eight days without eating?"

"Hardly. You woke up several times enough to take some food. Rest of the time, we gave you injections. You insisted on seeing Commander-in-Chief of the British Expeditionary Force, General Gort. You claimed you were a German prisoner and saw an important map. You were annoyed when we refused to summon the general and we gave you something to put you to sleep."

"It's all true, it's true," I said. "We were prisoners. We saw a map of the German invasion plan. We escaped to the Belgian lines in a plane we stole. Then a sergeant driving us to Namur was killed. We met some dispatch motorcycle riders. They were showing us the way to General Michiels' headquarters when the road exploded. It's all true. I'm telling you the truth."

The medical officer's eyes widened to the size of teacup saucers. He stared down at me and scratched his cheek with his index finger. "Okay lad, take it easy now. I guess you're not out of it yet. Lie back and—"

"I'm fine." I tried to shout, but it came out as a screech. "Honestly, it's all true."

The medical officer stared at me with his eyebrows squished together. Barney's voice echoed from the next bed. "Blimey, Archer. They said you were alright and then I guess I fell back asleep again. Is this a hospital? It's coming back to me now. Did we get blown up?"

The medical officer hurried over to Barney's bedside and inspected him.

Barney's face lit up. "Haven't I seen you before?"

"This morning," the medical officer said. "Looks like you're shipshape as well. But listen lad, do you also still insist on seeing General Gort?"

That question turned a magic key inside Barney. My English pal explained everything in much greater detail than I had.

"Yes sir," he finished up. "We have valuable information. If you could loan us a car, tell us where we can find the general, we'll get going right away."

"Ha!" the officer said with a stern look on his face. "After what you've been through? No chance. There may be something to all this, though. I'll get the general on the wire and inform him about you two. His headquarters isn't that far away. Perhaps he'll send one of his staff or even come himself. This whole thing is too fantastic. You're not trying to fool me now, are you?"

"On my word of honor, sir," Barney said in a solemn tone.

The medical officer hesitated a moment. He looked at Barney and me with his head tilted to the side and his lips pursed. Then he shrugged and slipped out of the ward.

I looked at Barney and grinned. "Glad you're not dead. Our nerve centers just got knocked around, but we could have been blown to bits. D'you know we've been here for eight days?"

Barney's jaw dropped. His eyes bugged out so far you

could knock them off like marbles on sticks. Then he flushed and laughed. "Come off it, Archer. Don't give me any of that. Eight days, no way."

"Not kidding. That's what he said." I gave Barney what I could remember of the medical officer's explanation. I wasn't even finished when the captain scrambled back into the ward. At his heels were two male orderlies. I broke off what I was saying and stared at the men. The medical officer drummed his foot against the floor. "Take them to my receiving office," he said to the orderlies and stepped to the side.

I didn't have a chance to ask any of the questions hovering on my lips. The orderlies snatched our beds and wheeled us down the aisle to the double doors. We passed through another ward and then rolled into a room that looked more like an office than a hospital room. After the orderlies left, the medical officer looked at us with a smile that reached his glossy eyes.

"I had no idea I had two young heroes under my charge. I thought you were just two lads caught up in the rush of things. General Gort is coming over now by car. He's heard all about you two."

I pushed myself up on my elbows. "About us? How could he have heard about us?"

"I believe it must've been through the Belgian high command," the medical officer said. "It seems a Belgian infantry lieutenant reported your flying incident to his commander. That information was passed until it reached General Michiels, who then contacted General Gort to see if you lads had gotten through."

The medical officer clasped his hands behind his back and continued. "That lieutenant didn't know what happened after you drove off in the scouting car with the sergeant. But I can assure you, General Gort is eager to meet you. He nearly broke my eardrums with all the shouting. I think you two lads are famous now."

"Blimey," Barney said with proper English modesty. "I bet anyone could've done it. And probably a much better job of it, too. Is it true, sir, that we've been here for eight days?"

The medical officer nodded. "Don't look so alarmed. That sort of thing isn't unusual. You're both safely out of it now. Another day or two of rest and all the food you can eat—you'll be good as new again."

"I'm feeling okay right now," I said. "There's something you didn't explain sir, how did we get here? Who found us?"

The medical officer shrugged. "That part is a bit sketchy. A Belgian ambulance driver stumbled across you two and realized you weren't dead and put you in his bus. His own hospital was being evacuated because of shell fire and continued westward. He reached our hospital and unloaded you two along with three other wounded Belgian gunners. And now, here you are. I wouldn't worry about it, just thank your lucky stars and let it be at that."

"Lucky stars?" I said. "Must be a million of them circling around me."

"We're in like one of those war movies or something," Barney said.

I grunted and shook my head. "A stupid bomb drops on me and I wake up hours later and miles away. Then a landmine or something blows up in my face, and I wake up eight days later, and who knows how far away. I guess I get around."

"Better not make a habit of it, lad," the medical officer said, snickering. "You know what they say about the third time."

The thought dawned on me. "What's happened in those eight days? Who's winning? Have the Allies stuck it to the Germans yet?"

The color from the medical officer's face drained. He let out a heavy sigh. He was about to speak when the office door swung open. A group of five tired-eyed British officers entered the room. A big man with greying, receded hair and steel-grey eyes led the party. His uniform was adorned with rows of decorations and ribbons. I knew instantly that this man was Commander-in-Chief, General Gort. The captain swung around and clicked his heels.

"There you are, sir," he greeted the general. "And here are your two young lads. This is the American chap, John Archer, and one of our own lads, Barney James."

The general turned his steel-grey eyes to Barney and smiled. "So you are the two, eh? I've heard quite a bit about you both. Who wants to talk first? I need to hear everything."

"Tell him all about it, Barney," I said. "You remember more about that map than I do."

Barney's chin dipped down and his ears turned a beet red. The general grinned and perched himself on the corner of the bed while his officers gathered around him. "Alright then Barney," the general said, "let's have it."

"Yes sir," Barney said. And he began talking in a low, clear voice.

14

I ZONED out as Barney recounted our experiences one by one. I was much more fascinated by staring at the British general. I'd seen General Gort's picture in the papers back home. He had a well-earned reputation as a fighter and a leader of men. And now, here he was, sitting a few feet from me.

This famous general was what a general should look like. Tall, lean, and a grim face etched in stone. The general leaned forward and made eye contact as Barney relayed our experiences. His steel-grey eyes locked onto Barney's lips to draw the words out faster. He stayed that way until Barney had spoken his last word. Then the general blew out a long breath and rubbed his hands together. "Well done, lads," the general spoke in a kind, soft voice that seemed strange coming from his stern face. "I'll make sure others hear this. You can mark my words. And you, America. John Archer. Can you add anything to the story?"

"Not much, General," I said, "except that Barney didn't tell you half of the things he did to get us out of jams. He—"

"Who got us out of that cell? Who flew that plane? Even though you crashed it and nearly broke our necks—"

I bit the inside of my cheek. "Because you're such a better

pilot? You almost killed us in that scouting car and drove on top of a landmine."

"Alright, alright," General Gort said. "Now, about that map, let's get back to that." The general nodded to one of his staff officers. A major whipped out a rolled map from under his arm and tossed it over. Another officer slid a table between the two beds. A third officer set down a handful of thumbtacks while the general unrolled the map and tucked it onto the flat table.

"This little village here." The general pointed with his stubby finger. "It's called Spontin. Do you remember if there was a colored pin there?"

I bent over and peered at the spot where the general had his finger. Barney answered first. "Yes, sir. A blue pin there. In fact, there were three blue pins on the line about a quarter of an inch apart. I'm sure I remember that."

"I see," the general said. "Do you recall if there was a date printed under these pins?"

"Yes," I interrupted. "May sixteenth. I'd bet on it."

"No need for that," the general said and slid his finger. "How about here? Vervins, France."

"Another blue pin there, sir," Barney said. "And the date marked under it was May eighteenth."

"And here at Guise?" General Gort slid his finger across the map again.

"I'm pretty sure that date was May nineteenth, sir," Barney said.

General Gort straightened up and glanced at his officers. They nodded almost in unison, their faces paled, and shoulders drooped. My body trembled. I tightened my stomach muscles to control the panic racing through me.

"This is the truth, General," I said. "I wouldn't make something like this up—"

General Gort shook his head and gave a ghost of a smile. "I believe you two saw the German plan of invasion."

"We could be a little mistaken about the dates, sir," Barney said in a voice laden with hesitation. "But I'm sure what we gave you was correct."

"You saw what the Germans planned to do." The general had a faint ironic edge to his voice. "We saw them do it. They took Spontin on the sixteenth. Vervins on the eighteenth, and Guise on the nineteenth. It's a matter of history now."

"Bloody hell!" Barney exclaimed. "They've taken that much, sir?"

General Gort lifted a tiny box from his pocket. He had a frown on his face. "I have a vital job for you two. Much depends on your memories. Here's a box of pins. I want you lads to put a pin on this map for every pin you saw at the Colonel's office. Colors don't matter. Study this map and revive your memories. Here are a couple of pencils to write as many dates as you can remember and put them under the right pins."

"General, there were over a hundred pins on that map," I said in a quivering voice.

"Stick the pins where you remember them—and the dates too," the general said. "Alright, we'll leave you to it."

Over an hour later, Barney and I leaned back from the map, mentally exhausted.

"Anything else would be a guess, sir," Barney said.

"Me too," I said. "That's all I can remember."

General Gort didn't answer. It was like he was made of solid granite. He leaned forward and put his elbow on the edge of the table. He cupped his broad chin in the palm of his hand. He was mesmerized moving from pin to pin on the map. The other officers waited like statues, not daring to even breathe. A silence hung over the room. I was tempted to yell, just to see what would happen. But I didn't let out a peep. I held my breath. Waiting like the others, motionless for the general to speak.

The general raised his head. "I will most certainly pass on the tales of your bravery. I know his Majesty King George will want to know. You've done a splendid job, lads. All England will be proud of you and—England never forgets."

"But sir," Barney said, looking down, his shoulders slumping. "If the Germans have advanced this far, what good is the information we've given you? We were too late."

"In war, it's never too late," the general said. "If I could've seen the map the way you did, things might be different. But even at that, you can't tell. No lad, the information has not come to me too late. In fact, it's come to me just in time. This information will save British and French Army lives."

The general got to his feet. He pushed up his shirt sleeves and inhaled deeply through his nose. "It depends on the Belgian King now," he said like he was talking to himself. "If he lets us down, exposes our left flank, it will be bad. But without this information, it could've been twice as bad."

"Then there is something to that rumor, sir?" the medical officer spoke up. "The Belgians might quit?"

"More than a rumor," the general said, his lips pressed into a thin white line. "Major Smith, bring this map along."

General Gort stood up and stepped closer to Barney and me. His staff officers clicked their heels and saluted. The general reached out his right hand. "Job well done, lads. I'm proud of you. Very proud. You'll hear more about this later."

I felt like I was in a trance as I watched the general and his staff officers sweep out of the room. We followed them to their cars outside. I stood at attention. Is this what it would be like in the Army? Standing and waiting around. I'd much rather be in Paris with Audrey talking about Charlie Chaplin movies at a café on Rue Crémieux.

"A red-letter day for you two," the medical officer said after the general and his officers rumbled away in their cars.

"So Captain, think we can get some food and our clothes back?" I asked.

"All the food you can eat," the medical officer said. "But no changing clothes. You two young heroes must stay in bed for a few more days, at least. And that's an order. I may not be a general, but I'm in charge of this hospital."

The medical officer meant what he said. Barney and I begged and pleaded to be allowed to get up, to help, to do anything. The hospital was shorthanded, and I was eager to do my part. Besides, staying in bed, trapped with my own thoughts, made me want to join the Army. It was a stupid idea. I couldn't make sense out of it. But I knew deep in the pit of my soul that I would fight. I didn't care about my safety. I'd even sacrifice Barney. But there needed to be a reckoning. These Germans could not be allowed to plow through Belgium and France—killing and murdering at will. Regardless of what General Gort said, we failed. We took too long to get our information into the right hands, and now so many people have suffered. How can I live with that? How can I help? How can we stop the Germans after they've smashed through France and Belgium? Now they're heading for the coast? My mind skipped from horrible to even more murderous scenario and back again. I must get out of this hospital and help.

The medical captain stuck to his order and would not let us go. On the second day after General Gort's visit, we were allowed to get up and wander around the hospital ward. The wounded soldiers complimented us on our brave and courageous work. But underneath the soldiers' admiration and attempts to be cheerful, there was a note of worry and strain. Like a slow dread creeping, reminding me of its presence by tumbling and grinding deep in the pit of my stomach.

We waited and waited. News of the battles sifted into the hospital wards. Exaggerated stories of Germans advancing through the papier mâché defense of the Allies only cut deep into the frayed nerves and tortured minds of the wounded men.

On the third day, it happened.

Belgium quit.

News spread like wildfire in the hospital ward. Misery and bitterness hung over every occupied hospital bed. The Belgians had given up and thrown down their guns. The whole left flank of the British Army was now exposed to the Germans racing down out of Holland. On the south, the French and British had been split by a German wedge driven straight across France to Abbeville on the channel coast. The entire British Army and part of the French were surrounded on three sides. Only one door of escape was left open. Dunkirk.

After that information sunk in, I grabbed Barney. We launched toward the medical captain's office. He was hanging up the telephone as we burst in. His hair was ruffled and greasy. Deep red circles ringed his eyes. He saw us and waved us inside.

"Well, how are the war heroes?" the medical officer said through a strained smile.

"Swell," I said.

"Fit, sir," Barney said.

The medical officer nodded and stared at us while drumming his fingers on top of the desk.

"You've heard the news, I take it?"

I nodded.

"We're in a tight spot," the medical officer said. "I've received orders to evacuate this hospital. There are over five hundred wounded men here and only a dozen ambulances. We're to evacuate at once to the base hospital at St. Omer. Now, lads, tell me the truth, do you really feel fit?"

"Captain, we can help," I said. "We both feel fit, honest."

"That's right, sir," Barney said. "What can we do?"

The medical officer let out a deep breath. "I don't have

enough ambulance drivers, and we must move the wounded from here at once. At the rate of speed the Germans are advancing, they'll be here by tonight."

I let out a soft gasp of air. "Tonight?"

"Hear those guns?" The medical officer nodded and held up a hand. "Less than twenty miles away and most definitely German. Gotta work fast, lads. Every man who doesn't leave here by tonight will become a German prisoner of war. I wouldn't ask you, except the situation is desperate. By rights, you should go along with the wounded instead of driving them."

"We're ready, sir," I said in a quiet voice. "What are your orders?"

The medical officer formed a steeple with his fingers and pressed them to his lips. "Change into your regular clothes. Then report to Lieutenant Dawson in the ambulance parking lot by the south wing. We'll meet again in St. Omer."

I shoved Barney into the doorway and then raced back to the ward for my clothes. The wounded soldiers hurled question after question at us. I didn't have time to answer any of them. I leaped into my clothes and hurried outside to meet Lieutenant Dawson.

Barney caught up to me as I turned the corner for the south wing. "I was afraid we'd get stuck in that bloody hospital for the rest of the war."

"Same here," I said. "I was afraid it was all over for us. But now I have a feeling this is just the beginning."

15

I YAWNED and lifted my head while mechanically reaching for the brake lever of the Daimler-built ambulance. I stared in the rearview mirror with bloodshot eyes at a scene that had become all too familiar. The dirt road wound away from the Lille hospital. Curved around the small pond and then disappeared from view into the woods less than a half-mile to the east.

How many times have I driven this road today? I don't know. Maybe a hundred? Fifty at least. My brain stopped thinking about things over two hours ago, and my actions have been mechanical. I'd help fill the ambulance at the hospital. Get behind the wheel, start the engine, take off the brake and shift into first gear. Then drive down that winding road, shifting into second and then into high. A stretch of brown road always in front of me. Driving forward. Dodging shell and bomb craters.

A deadly drone of Stuka dive bombers was getting closer. I pulled in under the nearest group of trees, tires screeching. I crouched at the wheel while death whistled down from the sky. Exploding onto the ground and spraying slivers of screaming steel in all directions. The smell of campfire and wounded men wafted into my nostrils. I climbed into the back of the ambulance after it was over and put a slipping bandage back in place. I lit a cigarette for a wounded soldier who didn't have the use of his hands. I grinned and said, "We'll be there soon, real soon."

I started on again and finally pulled back into the St. Omer hospital. I jumped out and helped unload and then crawled back in for a wild ride alone to Lille for another load of wounded men. Fifty trips? A hundred trips? I had no idea. Maybe I was on my one-thousandth trip. Am I dreaming? Am I asleep or awake? I'm not sure. My body stopped protesting all the aches and pains long ago. I didn't feel anything anymore. I only drove and drove and drove. Nothing else mattered except doing my share to make sure that not one wounded soldier got captured. I was in a race against the hordes of Nazi troops streaming across northern France and Belgium. The Germans raced to cut off the British from the last open channel port: Dunkirk.

I took off the emergency brake to start another trip. The passenger door flung open. I looked into a haggard, dirt-streaked face. "Barney? Are you tired of driving or what?"

"Let's go, Archer. This is the last load, and I'm riding with you. The captain and the staff are using my ambulance. I'm so tired."

"Right you are," I shifted the ambulance into first gear. "The last load. And it's just getting dark. We did it. The Nazis won't find anything here. Lean back and try to get a nap."

"What if you fall asleep at that wheel and tip us off into a ditch? No mate, I'll stay awake and try to keep you that way too. Archer, you made more trips than anyone. You want me to drive this one?"

"No way." I was laughing for the first time in hours. "I still remember you driving that Belgian scouting car. Negative, I'll do the driving. You relax. I'll be glad when this trip is over."

Barney stretched out his legs. "I think I'll sleep for another eight days, and I don't care what the bloody Nazis do about it."

We drove in silence for twenty minutes. I was so tired, too tired to talk. Besides, there was little to talk about except for our experiences on the road. Those we could save for another day. We still had this trip to finish. So we rode in silence. The sun slid down over the western lip of the world. I kept my headlights switched off until it was too dangerous to continue without them. The Luftwaffe had hammered the road all day long, and now it was pockmarked with shell craters. Trying to drive along in the dark would be suicide. Like trying to drive this ambulance over the edge of a cliff.

A dull rumble of guns echoed behind me. Punctuated now and then by a loud thunder of a landmine exploding. In the sky was the drone of planes, but they weren't close.

"Keep an eye out. I gotta keep these lights on, or we'll drive into a shell hole. If you hear something coming, yell, and I'll switch the lights off.

Barney stuck his head out the door window and looked up. "All clear so far."

A waving flashlight in the middle of the road caught my attention. I slipped the ambulance out of gear and steered around the rim of an angry bomb crater, and we rolled to a stop. A British infantry officer with a military police band on his sleeve ran to the ambulance and flashed his light in my eyes.

"Where you headed, son?"

"St. Omer," I said. "We're takin' the last load of wounded from the Lille hospital."

"You're not taking them to St. Omer no more," the officer said. "A mile up there, there's a road to the right. Take it and keep going until you get stopped. Whoever stops you will give you more directions. Alright, off with you. Good luck."

"Why not St. Omer?" I blurted out as the British officer was walking away. "We've been taking wounded there all day."

"I know," the British officer said in a half-bored-half-angry voice. "They've all been evacuated again to Dunkirk. The Nazis are in St. Omer. Better get a move on."

I slammed the ambulance back into gear and started off. My muscles quivered and I ground my teeth. I gripped the wheel so hard my hands hurt. Nazis are there? The Nazis are here! Nazis are everywhere. I glanced at Barney. His chin was firm with a defiant look in his eyes. But the droop of his shoulders betrayed the bitter thoughts that must be sweeping through his mind.

"Don't let it get you down," I said. "They'll knock Hitler and his Nazis back to Germany before it's over."

"I wasn't thinking of that. If we could have reached General Gort sooner."

"We did our best," I said in a firmer voice than I meant. "Besides, the general told us we helped him plenty. I don't think a man like General Gort sugarcoats his words to not hurt feelings. Here's the road. I wonder where it will take us."

We reached the turn off. A giant cluster of bomb craters littered the road in front of us. The Stukas must have had a heck of a time destroying this road. I detoured through fields to make the turn and got back onto the road. The next stretch of road was barely touched by bombs, and we sped up our ambulance. The good road brightened my spirits, boosted my morale—the fatigue was washing away. Or was this my 104th wind? Barney still gazed through the windshield at the glow of headlights on the road. But his body had straightened up a bit. He had a less depressed air about him.

But it was like all this had been planned by the fates controlling the war. Our immediate destinies. Every time something went our way, an equally worse thing waited to crash into us. And not a mild setback. Something horrible and deadly. I'm a long way from my Paris hotel and wish I was back there now with my feet up and Audrey across the table from me.

My first sign that we were in trouble came as we roared around a bend in the road. The road straightened out like an arrow. I stiffened up in my seat and pointed. "It looks like an earthquake hit here."

Both sides of the road were strewn with heaped war wreckage. Machine guns and howitzers lay scattered. Flipped ammunition wagons spilled their contents on the ground like sand from a box. Shell blasted tanks rested on soft ground at crazy angles. Some of them were blown wide apart, and all of them, no use to anyone.

"Like driving through a junkyard." I slowed down our ambulance. "What do you think happened? That's all British. See the markings?"

"Looks like a retreating British column caught by bombers. See where the craters were filled so the rest could carry on. What equipment they couldn't take, they must've destroyed." Barney pointed to another man with a flashlight up ahead. "He's English."

A khaki-clad figure with an MP band on his arm stood in the middle of the road. I slipped our ambulance out of gear and let it roll to a stop. I stuck my head out the window. "We've got wounded here," I said as another British officer walked toward us. "They turned us off onto this road, a few miles back. Told us the next officer would give us more instructions."

"More wounded?" The officer said in a low-pitched voice. "I doubt if there'll be more room. But go ahead. First turn take a left and two miles straight after. There's a railroad junction there, and still working. At least I hope so. They'll take your men on board. Along with you now."

"What happened here?" I reached for the gear shift lever.

"It was the worst," the officer said with a vacant stare and gestured with his hand. "Stukas got an entire battalion. A nasty business. Now get going, you hear me?"

I wasn't going to argue with him. I lurched our ambulance forward and kept my eyes open for the turn to the left. After I found it and turned off, it was more or less untouched by bombs so I could keep my speed up. Soon after, we came to an army of British soldiers. They clogged the road and overflowed on both sides. Hundreds of pairs of eyes turned toward us as our headlights cut through the night. A soldier with sergeant chevrons on his sleeves rushed up to us.

"Shut off those bloody lights, you fool. You want those Jerry planes to—what's going on here?"

"We got wounded from Lille sergeant," Barney called out. "The officer back there told us to take them to the rail junction. How far is it?"

"More wounded?" the sergeant said through his teeth, his jaw clenched. "Keep going. You're practically there, mates."

The sergeant stepped back and cupped his hands to his mouth. "Make way!" he shouted along the road choked with British troops. "Ambulance coming through. Make way there you blokes. Ambulance coming through. Give them the horn lads, that'll make them jump."

I started our ambulance forward at a crawl and held my hand on the horn. The sergeant's voice boomed behind us. Barney got out on the running board and started shouting, "Make way for the ambulance," at the top of his voice. For a few awful seconds, I was afraid the soldiers wouldn't move, but shouting the word "ambulance" did the trick. They shuffled off to both sides and left a path for us down the middle of the road. I drove with one hand on the wheel and the other on the horn. I steered the ambulance down a path until a bomb-shattered railroad bridge stopped us—no need to go farther from here.

We'd reached the rail junction, or what was left of it. Eastward from the bridge, the track was a puzzle of twisted steel.

But westward from the bridge had hardly been touched. A long train of twenty cars were on the track with the engine at the far end. Dim lights moved around all over the place like fireflies on a muggy night. A murmur of voices filled the air. Long lines of battle-weary soldiers climbed into railway cars. A squad of soldiers with white bands on their sleeves swooped down on us.

"Shut off your motor, mate," a voice shouted. "You won't be needing it anymore. Step lively, lads. Easy with those poor blighters, now. That's the way."

Before Barney and I could climb stiff-legged down from the ambulance, the white-banded group of soldiers held the rear doors open. They gently but swiftly lifted the wounded onto stretchers and carried them onto the train. No one spoke. Even the wounded were silent. All that counted from here was speed. I watched for a minute then went up to the soldier who'd given the orders.

"Where's the train going?"

"Dunkirk, unless Jerry flyers try to stop us," the soldier replied without looking at me. "Any more of these chaps coming along behind you?"

"This is the last load from Lille," I said. "Don't know if there are others."

"Lille?" The soldier jerked his head back. "I thought the Jerries were there?"

"I bet they are now," Barney said. "Room enough for us on this train, you think?"

"Always room for two more on anything." The soldier watched the stretchers disappear into the maze of moving lights. "You lads follow me, and I'll—"

The soldier never finished the rest of his sentence. If he did, I didn't hear him. A drone of engines high in the sky to the east dominated my attention. Like a thousand men put whistles to their lips and blew them at the same time.

"Bombers!" a voice roared through the foghorn.

"Everyone aboard," bellowed another.

"Never mind your bloody kit, get aboard," a third man thundered.

"All lights out," a fourth voice carried above the others.

The moving lights turned off. Everything plunged into darkness. Darkness coupled with the throbbing beat of approaching airplanes ahead. Barney and I ran toward the train. We ran smack into a wall of solid flesh. We tried to force our way through, but it was like trying to push a tidal wave to one side. We weren't the only ones trying to board that train. A few hundred others had the same idea.

The train's shrill whistle cut through the other sounds. Seconds later, an angry roar from hundreds of throats signaled the train was moving. We stopped trying to push our way forward. And stood there listening to the angry shouting of the troops who couldn't get aboard. The sound of the train as it clacked on the track, picking up speed to race east.

"Here they come. Scatter!"

Maybe it was the same foghorn voice, maybe not. Everyone heard the command and bolted. The air ricocheted with a howl of diving wings. I thought of that bomb blasted bridge. The road once dipped under it, but now it was a cave made from jagged chunks of stone with twisted steel rails and splinter ties for roof shingling. I grabbed Barney by the arm and spun him.

"That busted bridge," I shouted in his ear. "We can crawl under it. Should be safe there."

Barney's eyes widened and he nodded.

The leading Stuka bomber dropped low, released its load, and screamed high into the night sky. Its bomb struck one-hundred yards away, but the concussion lifted me off my feet. I sprinted through the roaring darkness and barely avoided turned over trucks and hunks of the bombed out station by inches. I leaped and scrambled down under the bridge into a cave-like hole that had been blown out of the supporting walls. With Barney behind me, we crawled back over the broken stones as far as we could. We sat huddled together, listening to the apocalypse.

"We got a load of wounded on that train," I shouted through a lull in the mayhem. "That's something, at least."

"We did our best," Barney said, sagging back against the wall. "I'm tired. Stukas or not. I can't stay awake another minute."

His words touched something inside me. My mind and body went limp. I battled to keep my eyes open. To keep lookout in case we had to change our shelter. But it was like a ton of weights hung on my eyelids. Impossible to keep them open any longer. Above our heads, the world exploded with fire and flame. Underneath us shook and shivered as each devastating blow struck. None of it reached us. We'd taken an awful beating for hours and our bodies needed rest. Even though the world outside was coming to an end, it had no effect on Barney and me because we were both asleep.

16

THE COLD, clammy air of early dawn pried my eyelids open—I returned to the conscious world.

Massive grey shadows surrounded me. The shadows, most of them, were rocks and huge chunks of cement. Light filtered down through the cracks and holes between them. That realization brought me back to where I was. I followed the last memory of all that had happened. I pushed myself to my feet. My movements woke Barney, slumped against a rock. He groaned and opened his eyes and stared blankly around. Then he sat up and flexed his arms and legs.

"Morning," I said. "The Stukas are gone. Let's get out of here and see if we can board that train." The aches and pains rolled through my stiff body. "I can barely move my arms and legs. So stiff."

"I never thought a bloke could fall asleep while bombs were falling," Barney said. "My father told me he once slept through a ten-hour bombardment in the Somme River valley back in nineteen seventeen. I always thought he lied. But now—Wait, what's that?"

I swiveled to listen to the strange sound. "Troops marching. The train must be back. Come on, come on, Barney."

I scrambled forward and crawled up out of the cave between rocks onto firm ground. I glanced through a crack that gave me a clear view of the road running along the back of the bomb-shattered station. My belly fluttered and turned into a sudden and uncomfortable coldness. Barney bumped into me from behind. I whirled around and put a finger to my lips.

I pointed with my other hand for him to look through the crack in the rocks. Barney squirmed past me and peered through the gap. His body stiffened, a sharp sound of sucking air into his lungs. He turned around and stared wide-eyed at me while he licked his lower lip.

"Germans," he whispered. "The Nazis are all over the place. We've been left behind, Archer. Our mates moved on after the Stukas left. We were asleep."

"How many of them are there? What are we supposed to do from here?"

"I don't know. We should stay where we are," Barney said through trembling lips, his shoulders tight. "There's gotta be thousands of them out there."

I took another look through the crack and gulped. "More like millions. Last thing I want to be is a German prisoner—again. Okay, let's stay right here."

"We won't starve, no matter how long they take to march through," Barney said. "We both have plenty of chocolate bars from the hospital. I still have plenty of water in my canteen. You?"

"It's full." I patted my canteen at the end of the strap hooked over my shoulder. "Plenty of chocolate and water. But I hope they don't stick around too long, or we'll never get out of here. Maybe we were crazy to hide here."

Barney pulled a chocolate bar from his pocket. "At least we didn't get hit with any bombs."

I crinkled my lips and didn't want to think about how lucky we actually were. "I hope those British troops got away. I guess they must've, or we'd hear the fighting." I rested the side of my head on my palm.

Barney looked at me and, through a mouthful of crunching chocolate bar, asked, "What's the matter?"

I exhaled a deep breath. "We started this business behind German lines, and now here we are back again. I hope we don't end up that way. Wonder how long we'll have to wait this one out. At least until it's dark."

Barney crawled up the stones and peered through the crack. When he came back down, he slumped against a rock. "At least until dark. I heard more war music and saw them wheeling some guns into position back by the railroad station. I think they're planning to stay here a while."

"When it gets dark, we're out of here," I said in a sober voice. "Guns or no guns."

As if our silence was a signal to the gunners above, the earth and sky shook and trembled. Gun muzzles belched out sheets of flame and steel-clad missiles screaming off to the east. We crawled farther back into the cave and hunkered down to get away from the jolting and hammering and pounding.

Seconds ticked into minutes, and minutes ticked to hours. Two hours, then three, then four. I double-checked my watch to make sure it still worked. The guns hammered and snarled and pounded away at their distant objectives. It seemed like it would never end. We tried to steel ourselves against the thunder and shaking and heaving of the earth underneath us. My eardrums ached and were ready to burst. We tore off pieces of our shirts and use them as plugs to stuff in our ears. While that helped some, it made speech between us impossible.

The roaring, barking thunder lasted all afternoon. Toward evening it died down. When the shadows of night crept up, it stopped altogether. We crawled forward onto the bomb-made rock steps and peered through the crack again between the stones. The guns were not being hooked onto the tractors. Nor were the swarms of troops climbing onto the long lines of motorized Panzer tanks and trucks. Mess wagons were being rolled forward. We crouched and watched. A smothering feeling felt like it was choking me. My spirit sank when the fluttering flare lights lit above our heads. A sudden terror gripped over me. I grabbed Barney's arm, and we scrambled deep back into our hiding place.

Barney ran his hand over a hardened surface that would be his bed for another night. "Maybe we'll get lucky, and they'll pull out before dawn. Or maybe in the morning, for sure."

As if the gods of war heard Barney's words and laughed out loud with a wicked joy. The Germans didn't leave during the night. Nor did they leave in the morning. At dawn, they started their bombardment again. And for another entire day, we huddled together in our hiding place. We struggled with every bit of our willpower to stop from going stark-raving-mad from the thunder of their guns.

Then, with less than an hour of daylight left, the guns fell silent. Sounds of feverish activity, guttural orders in German flew thick and fast. Tractor engines roared. Truck transport gears wrenched in a nerve-rasping-grinding sound. We watched through our lookout crack as the Germans puttered off down toward the southwest. Neither of us spoke until the last truck passed from view. By then, it was pitch dark, and the Germans were only a shimmering red glow to the east and the south.

"Let's get going before the others come," I said. "Which way should we head?"

"The railroad track," Barney said after a moment of silence. "It must have been blown to bits by the Stukas, or else a train would have taken the Germans away. I think they headed southwest."

"That track is supposed to lead to Dunkirk. I hope the British are still there."

"They must be. You can still hear the guns up ahead, so there must be someone besides Germans around. Look at that fog, or is it even fog? It's raining. We're lucky, we won't be seen or heard so easily now. Come on Archer, let's bloody well get on with it. Like the blokes in the RAF say, Tally-ho."

"Tally-ho," I said in my worst English accent and scrambled up behind Barney out of the cave.

We walked side-by-side on the single track with sharp eyes to avoid tumbling into a bomb crater. After a few hundred yards, the railroad track became a long stretch of twisted steel and pulverized ties. But even though the roadbed was pockmarked with bomb craters, it served as an eastward guide.

Layers of fog rolled in from the east. With every step, a chilling rain sprayed down on us. But instead of being annoyed and uncomfortable. The miserable weather gave me hope. An added protection from German patrols. It hid us from the rest of the world. We trudged and stumbled along the bomb-blasted strip of railroad tracks. The stench of burned metal gunpowder lingered in the air. The dazzling glow of red to the south iced my heart. All that sound to the south must mean the Germans had not cut off the retreating armies at Dunkirk. Does that mean fifty-thousand British soldiers were attacking the Germans at Douai and Canal de Bergues? Were they going to sacrifice themselves for the three hundred and thirty thousand other British soldiers to escape to England?

Our steps were in sync and we picked up the pace. The hope of somehow getting through this mess lifted my spirits. We'd find a way to get through the darkness. We'd get to England ourselves and then get some payback. What am I thinking? We're not in this war. What if I joined up with the English and volunteered? Maybe since we're heroes, they'll let me pilot one of their RAF Spitfires or Hurricanes. The hope of somehow getting through this and getting some payback was my fuel. Not hate, but love. Love for all the innocent, helpless people who can't protect themselves. Love for the beautiful free land and the right for people to live their way.

On we went in the darkness. We stumbled over rocks and metal objects. We tripped into bomb craters and thumped our shins. Bumps and bruises screamed at me in painful bites on my body. We continued moving forward. We stopped talking to conserve energy. We had no idea how many miles of bomb-blasted roadbed lay ahead of us. The fog and rain dulled the sound of the guns. We couldn't tell if we were drawing closer or heading away from them.

Although I looked at it a million times, the dull red glow ahead always remained the same. Never once brightened or faded. I felt like a horse pulling a mill. Walking, walking, walking, yet never seeming to get anywhere. Never seeing anything different to give us proof we covered any ground. Every piece of twisted track we stumbled over was the same as the last. Every bomb crater we sprawled into was no different from the others. Darkness, fog, and the shimmering red glow were always the same in the next second, the next minute, and the next hour.

I was determined to not give up. I forced myself forward, foot after foot, yard after yard, and mile after mile. Nothing but a fierce burning flame drove our tired legs and bodies forward. Then the world shattered in an explosion of sound. It felt like an eternity passed before the sound connected to my brain. Then I realized nothing had exploded. It was a loud voice, less than ten feet in front of us.

"Halt!"

That voice shattered my hopes. It gripped my heart with fingers of ice and drained every drop of blood from my body. Fate was laughing at me. The one thing I dreaded most had now come to pass. We'd stumbled headlong into a nest of Germans.

"Halt, you blighters, 'fore I run my bayonet through your bellies."

The truth crashed home. I pressed my palms to my eyes and laughed like I'd just heard-the-funniest-joke-of-my-life. The voice was speaking in *English*.

17

"Wait, wait mate," Barney's voice cried out in the darkness. "We're not bloody Germans. He's an American and I'm English. Are we near Dunkirk?"

A tiny beam from the flashlight caught us in its glow through the rain and fog. The light struck, and there was a gasp of dumbfounded amazement.

"Bloody hell," said the voice in the back of the light. "What are you young lads doing out here? And where in the bloody hell did you come from?"

The flashlight lowered, and in a dim outline was a British soldier. His gas mask and ration kit were slung over his shoulder, and he carried a rifle with a wicked-looking bayonet.

"We're trying to reach Dunkirk," Barney said. "We've been hiding at a railway junction called Niort, I think. Part of the sign was blown away, but I think that's what it was called."

"Niort?" The British officer said. "Come off it now, lad. If you were at Niort, how did you get here? I suppose by a bleeding train, eh?"

"No, we walked," I said, "along what was left of the railroad. We missed the last train two nights ago. It pulled out in a hurry when the Stukas came."

The British soldier whistled through his teeth and then flashed his light on us again. "How can you beat that. You lads were left behind and had to march all the way with Jerry throwing everything he had at you. You know how far you two nippers have walked?"

"The way I feel," I said, "about a million miles."

"More like eighteen or nineteen, lad," the British soldier said, and laughed. "But that ain't half of it. You walked right through the German line. Right through their bleeding lines, and then not knowing about it. Now mate, this is a tale to tell the lads at the pub if I ever get back home."

"But how far are we from Dunkirk?" I asked. "Is there any way to get there besides walking? I don't want to walk another step."

The British soldier jerked his thumb over his shoulder. "See them flames? That's Dunkirk. About two miles. It's time for me to go in from my patrol. I got a motorbike and a sidecar over there. You lads can ride in the car, but we better get on it. It's almost dawn, and the Stukas will come to raise another round of hell soon. But wait a minute, lads. Who are you, and what were you doing at Niort? You're not even in uniform?"

"This is John Archer, an American," Barney said. "My name is Bernard James. We've been trying to get back to England for days, and—"

"What's that?" the British soldier said, his eyes glowing. "Archer and James? The American and English lads who stole a plane and all the rest with it? Why didn't you say so? You two are heroes. The whole Army's been talking about what you two did. Come on then. If anyone's gonna get a boat ride back home, it's you two. I'm so anxious to get back home, I'm ready to swim that bloody channel orders or no orders. Come on then."

The British soldier grabbed us both by the arm and hurried us through the dark to the right. He must've known the way well because we didn't bump into a single thing. When he let go of us, he jumped into some bushes. He was out in no time pushing out an army motorcycle and a sidecar. He slung his rifle over his shoulder and straddled the seat.

"Hop in, lads," he barked and kicked the engine to life. "Hang on for your lives. The beach where they're taken them off onto the ships is on the far side of town. But the whole bloody town's on fire. We gotta go through it. Here we go, and a double-double to the blasted Jerries."

Barney and I wedged ourselves into the sidecar. The British soldier took off in such a dash he practically rode right out from underneath us. Yelling any complaints would've just been a waste of breath. Besides, the British soldier wouldn't have been able to hear us over the roar of the engine. I concentrated on trying to stay in the sidecar, hoping he was an expert driver.

He was more than that. He raced through the darkness without slowing his speed. The rain drizzled down on the street, glistening in the faint glow of dim light. It looked slippery, like black ice, and a hundred times I closed my eyes, waiting for a sickening crash that never came. When I dared to open them again, we hurtled forward, making as much noise as a division of tanks.

We covered the two miles to Dunkirk in about as many minutes. Through the last hundred yards, the fog ended, and the rain passed on behind us. I looked ahead and caught my breath in a gulp. Dunkirk rose like a wall of orange flame and billowing smoke towering high into the sky. It was like I walked out of a dark room into the open mouth of a blast furnace. I cast a quick glance at the British soldier on the motorcycle, half expecting to see an expression of alarm and dismay passing across his unshaven face. But I saw nothing. The British soldier lowered his head, and the corners of his eyes tightened.

"Hang on, lads," he shouted, just loud enough for me to

understand, without taking his eyes off the road. "Here comes the first of it."

We charged toward a burning building. Barney and I ducked our heads like the soldier did. In a split second, we had the sensation of hurtling straight across the mouth of a boiling volcano that shot up tongues of flame on all sides.

"Lean to the right," the British soldier yelled.

We leaned together, and the motorcycle and sidecar careened around the corner of the street. It hesitated halfway around and we slid, but our driver checked the slide with a vicious twist of the wheel, and we went roaring up a smoke-filled street. Seconds later, our driver yelled for us to lean again. We did. We leaned more than a dozen times in the next few minutes. All the while, the heat of the flames roasting us from all sides. The crash of falling walls and bombs exploding left a tightness in my chest and a rushing sound ringing in my ears.

We shot through the middle of the last wall of fire and burst out onto a stretch of hard-packed sand. Several seconds ticked by before the heat faded, and I felt a rain-soaked salt air strike my face. I swallowed clean air into my lungs with a gulping, gasping sound. A squad of British soldiers rose out of the sand in front of us. Our driver stood up on his footplates and roared above the sound of his engine.

"Out-of-the-way," he shouted. "A couple young heroes coming through."

British soldiers leaped to the side as we charged through without a single check on our speed. Maybe the soldiers heard him, or maybe they didn't want to get run over by an onrushing motorcycle. After a few hundred more yards, the soldier cut his engine, slammed on his brake, and slid around, sending a shower of wet sand flying.

"There you are, lads," he shouted and bolted from the seat. "How's that for a bit of a joyride? She's a good little ride, she is. A bit slow, but she'll do. Now, wait here a minute while

I go see if the commandant's about. Sit tight, lads. I'll be right back."

He raced off to the left. Barney and I sat there in silence. We fought to get control of our breathing and unwedge ourselves from the sidecar. When we hobbled down onto the sand, I felt myself all over to make sure my arms and legs hadn't been left behind.

"Our Belgian sergeant was a beginner compared to that guy," I said. "He went through some of those buildings instead of around. Look at those flames. The whole town is going up in smoke."

Barney grabbed my arm and pointed with his other hand. "Look toward the beach. It's the British Army. They're wading out to get to the boats. Must be too shallow for them to get any closer. Going home, mate. Going home." Barney's voice took on a higher pitch and a breathless quality. His face and neck flushed with a reddish color.

I stared at the grotesque glow of the burning channel. Boats of every type littered the horizon. Rowboats and sailboats. Fishing smacks and pleasure yachts. Coastal vessels and ferry boats. Motorboats and canoes. Barges and British destroyers. Anything and everything that could float had been brought over to help in the evacuation. The British Navy was taking the British Army home. All of England had come to rescue her men.

It was the most selfless thing I'd ever seen in my life. A sudden chill rushed through my body. I rubbed at the visible gooseflesh on my arms and shivered. The entire beach was covered with row upon row of British and French soldiers. They stood in long columns of ten and twelve men across. Columns stretched from high on the beach to far out into the shallow water. Cars, tanks, and trucks, anything on wheels, had been driven out into the water and parked side-by-side to form a pier that could reach out into deeper water. But there were only a few of those piers. Most of the men waded out in the water until it rose to their chests and necks.

Barney and I stood like tree stumps, wide-eyed at the sight that will forever exist in my memory. While my eyes soaked up the scene, my ears tickled with the hodgepodge of sound. All the sounds came from offshore. The blast of whistles, the blowing of signal horns, the roar of engines. Shouts from the appointed and self-made skippers and crews of the fantastic rescue fleet. The troops hardly made a sound. Maybe they were too tired. Maybe the roar of battle still rampaged through their ears. Maybe they were content to follow the next man and hope they'd be taken aboard some kind of boat and sail away before the Stukas returned. But I bet the real reason for their silence was because most of them had been there for days waiting their turn, dodging Stuka bombs and bursting shells. And after that ordeal, they were too stunned to know or even care about talking. I think each man had a single, all-important goal. Get on a boat. And they slogged and sloshed toward it, numb to all that was going on around them.

"It's . . . It's like this isn't real," I whispered. "It's like being at a movie and seeing something you know is made up. There's gotta be thousands of them. Thousands. I wonder how many have gotten off already? And—"

I froze. Above the crackling and sullen roar of the flames devouring the city came that dreaded sound. Like the drumming moan of a night wind in the trees. But it wasn't. It was a sound that chilled the blood of every man onshore and off. It was Luftwaffe Stukas and Heinkels and Messerschmitts coming up along the horizon of the rising dawn. A long second passed before the planes were drowned out by groans and curses welling up in the throats of thousands of soldiers. None of the men broke ranks. Everyone stayed in their place. Like they were on the parade ground instead of a beach strewn with their own dead. Soldiers unslung and pointed rifles and machine guns at the fast-moving planes, but no man gave up his place in line.

And then those winged vultures under Göring's command came howling down out of the sky. Their noise drowned out all other noises, including the noise of the guns that received them. It was as if a giant tore the roof off the top of the world. It wasn't a scream, and it wasn't an earth-trembling wail, nor was it a continual thunderous roar. It was a sound never heard before and may never be heard again. A mighty collection of all the sounds in the universe blended into one titanic inferno of noise.

Barney and I stood hypnotized. It didn't occur to me to run for shelter. Our feet were lumps of lead on the ground of a great magnet that held us tight. Orange and red flame spewed up a couple hundred yards away from us. A bomb exploded, but I couldn't hear the sound. Another fountain of flame and sand showered down over everything. But no individual sound of a bomb going off. Part of the sky turned into a raging ball of red fire. I looked upward in time to see a Heinkel bomber outlined in livid flame. Then it was swallowed by that flame and plunged down into the offshore water and disappearing as if by magic.

It was then I realized that not all the planes were German. British Hurricanes, Spitfires, and Defiants dropped out of the dawn sky in groups of three to pounce on the enemy planes in a relentless, furious attack. The Royal Air Force was outnumbered. One British plane against five Germans, against ten, or even fifty. The British pilots fought impossible odds. They sacrificed themselves to save British troops on the beach. Wave after wave of German planes shot up the trapped soldiers like cattle. The RAF flew into the fight, acting as a buffer to save the beached troops. A feeling of weightlessness swelled through me. A tingling surged from my chest and spread outward like an explosion of heat. I would be a pilot. I would sacrifice myself, if necessary, to save others. I now know what I was put on this earth to do.

My right arm throbbed. Barney gripped it with one hand and pounded it with his other fist. His eyes were bloodshot and crazed like a madman. After getting my attention, he stopped pounding and pointed left beyond the short line of bomb blasted wharves.

"Archer," he shouted. "Look at that first wharf. A motor-boat. A Messerschmitt sprayed the lad at the wheel. He's trying to get up, but he's pinned down. Can you swim? We gotta reach that boat before it hits the rocks. Look, the Messerschmitt's shooting again."

While Barney screamed in my ear, I looked out at the boat. A long, slinky looking powerboat that wasn't slinking along anymore. The lone figure collapsed across the engine hood, and a diving Messerschmitt hammered more bullets into his body. A running tide carried the craft broadside toward jagged rocks that stuck up out of the water less than two-hundred yards away.

I gazed at the boat, forgetting to blink. Then I realized that my feet were pounding across the beach. I raced toward the water's edge. I glanced over my shoulder and saw Barney James was close on my heels.

18

By the time I reached the water, I'd already stripped off my jacket and flung my canteen away. Shoulder to shoulder, Barney and I splashed out as far as we could and then dived in. We struck out for the helpless craft drifting toward doom from the tide. Above us raged another battle. Bombs fell close. When one struck the water and went off, it felt like a thousand fists hammered against my chest. Behind us, the flames of Dunkirk soared. The glow in the water looked like we swam in an ocean of blood. Ahead of us was the sleek looking motorboat, drifting on the crest of a shimmering red sea.

A fire burned in my lungs. My arms were like bars of lead that took every ounce of my remaining strength to lift and cut down into the water. I fought back the aches, the pains, and the nibbling fatigue. I fixed my eyes on that drifting motorboat, and I didn't move them until, after what seemed like years, I was there alongside it. I hooked an arm over the side of the gunwale. For a moment, I hung there panting and gasping for air. Then, at an unspoken signal, Barney and I shifted our grip to the small brass rail that ran along each side from stem to stern and hauled ourselves onto the boat.

We didn't speak a word to each other. Words were unnecessary now. We had a job to do. A job to be done fast. Those rocks were less than sixty yards away. I shook the water from my face and leaped toward the engine hood, lifted the bullet-ridden body, and lowered him gently to the deck. Barney snatched up an oar and rushed toward the bow to fend off the rocks.

I lifted the engine hood and took one look inside. A sudden lightness flashed through me, and a mountain of tension disappeared. The Messerschmitt bullets hadn't touched the American-built engine. A quick glance down at the priming can in the dead man's stiff hand told me he was trying to start the engine when the Messerschmitt first dived. Maybe he throttled too much and stalled the engine. If something else was wrong, and the priming can didn't do the trick, then Barney and I could at least save the boat from being slammed up against the rocks.

We needed Lady Luck to shine on us once again. I primed the engine and stepped on the starter pedal. The engine roared up instantly in her full-throated song. I vaulted for the wheel, yanked back on the throttle, and then swung the wheel over hard. The rudder bit into the water, and the powerboat gently kissed the jagged rocks before gliding out into deeper water. I caught my breath and stuck my head over the starboard side. Our powerboat had an angry scratch, but she was still seaworthy.

A steel Nazi fish slipped past a destroyer. They fired a torpedo into the maze of craft hovering offshore beneath a ferocious sky battle. The torpedo streaked out from its tube and slammed into the bow of a coastal vessel plodding out to the center of the channel. A blaze of light gushed up from the ship's side, crowded with khaki-clad soldiers. I lost my view as the vessel heeled over and engulfed in a gigantic cloud of smoke. I hauled down hard on the wheel and pulled our motorboat's bow away from shore and out toward that floating cloud of smoke and dull red flame.

Other boats did the same, but we were closer than any others to reach them. I reduced speed and worked our boat inch by inch toward the cluster of heads bobbing out from under the edge of a cloud of smoke. When I was close enough, I throttled all the way back and let go of the wheel, and raced with Barney to the stern of the boat. We grabbed the first hand stretched up toward us and pulled the dripping bodies into the boat. No sooner were they in when we felt a shift and grabbed for the next outstretched hand. Then another, and another, until there were no more bobbing heads close to us.

Another craft arrived and picked up survivors from the doomed ship. I straightened up and stared out across the water in time to see the last bit of the torpedoed ship's bow slide down below the waves and disappear. Where was that U-boat? If one slipped past, then why not two or three? Dunkirk was behind us and the sky battle raged, but I didn't know what lurked in the waters underneath. I needed to get this boat away and quick for all concerned.

I reached the wheel the same time Barney did. Hardly realizing it, we both took hold of it. I shot out my hand and opened up the throttle, and as one person, we guided the powerboat in and around the other rescue craft heading out into the channel. Once nothing but open water waited ahead of us, my knees buckled on my wobbly legs, and I flopped down on the deck of our boat and laughed out loud.

"That better be the last surprise," I said. "Not like anything else could surprise me now."

Barney let out a huge breath and slumped down next to me. "I think the excitement's over for us now, mate. In another hour, we'll be in England."

A powerful hand clapped my shoulder. A hoarse voice boomed, "Well, of all things. You two again?"

I recognized that voice and spun around. My jaw fell open, and my neck tipped back. Standing in his water-soaked uniform was General Gort, commander of the British Expeditionary Force. His piercing grey eyes bored into mine, his face a mask of white teeth and a wide smile.

"General," I said and swallowed to relieve the dryness from my wide-open mouth. "I didn't know we hauled you aboard."

"But you did, and I thank you for that," the general said. "And you know the strangest thing, I was just telling the captain of the boat how you stole that plane, right when the blasted torpedo struck. It's incredible. How in the world did you get here? And in this boat?"

"General, sir, if you don't mind. We'll tell you all about it later," Barney spoke up and put a hand on the general's sleeve. "Please tell us the truth. We've got to know. Did the information we gave you earlier help? Did you get it too late?"

General Gort glared at Barney and then shook his head. "Back there is the last of the British Army to leave France." The general pointed at the beach at Dunkirk. "We've been getting them out for days against impossible odds. The only reason I was on that torpedoed boat instead of being back there to the last man was that I had orders to return to England at once. They will all be back in England before this fog lifts and gives the Stukas the chance they want. What I'm trying to tell you is this: if I'd not received your information in time, thousands of those brave lads would never have reached Dunkirk in time to be taken off. They'd be trapped in France and Belgium. No, lads, it was not too late, and you two are owed a debt of gratitude from England."

"I'm glad it wasn't too late," I said. I tried to say more, but I had no words.

Barney shouted in a choked voice, "Dover!" Tears trickled down his cheeks. "The white cliffs of Dover. England."

"Yes, the cliffs of Dover, in England," General Gort said. We took a beating in France, but it's far from over. We may lose more battles. Maybe several. But in the end—we will win. We must win. There must always be an England. Always.

Three days later, I sat in the sitting room of Barney James's house on Baker St. In London. My father and Audrey were with me. Within less than an hour after touching down on English soil, the British War Office alerted my father, who'd flown back to Paris looking to pick up the trail of his missing son. He met Audrey waiting in that Paris hotel and brought her along. Now, the three of us sat with Barney and his father waiting for General Gort. We'd received a message that the general was on his way there and for us to await his arrival.

"I wish he'd hurry," I said. "This anticipation is making me crazy."

"So, he didn't say what he wanted? Only that he wanted to see us?" Barney asked his father for the third time in an hour.

Barney's father shook his head. "No, Barney. He didn't say a word about it."

"I think I know what it is," I said and rubbed the back of my neck. "He fixed it up for us to get into the RAF, even though we're still underage. He said he'd do everything he could. And Dad?"

Douglas Archer looked into his son's face, and raised his eyebrows.

"I hope you're going to be okay with it," I said. "I mean getting into the RAF if I can. It's . . . it's just that it's so important now. I gotta help these people fight the Nazis. I want to help, no matter what kind. They need me. They need my help."

"I know how you feel," my father said with a frown, like he'd seen a ghost. "I felt the same way twenty-three years ago. Stay over here and help, son. Just try to not get yourself killed."

A loud knock on the door nearly took my breath away. Barney's father answered it and came back into the room with General Gort. The general greeted us all and then handed Barney and me each a small box.

I opened my box and gasped. A Victoria Cross inscribed with the words *For Valour* rested inside each box.

"Is this what I think it is?" I asked.

"Yes, and congratulations, lads," the general said. "There's another reason I came here today. Their Majesties, King George and Queen Elizabeth, are waiting to receive you at Buckingham Palace. This is the highest honor a King's subject can receive. The last time a civilian was awarded a Victoria Cross was in 1879."

"The king," Barney said in a high pitched, squeaky voice. "And queen."

"Whoa, meeting the king and queen in Buckingham Palace," I said. "I'm honored General, but I have to know. What Barney and I asked you about . . . the RAF. Do we have a chance?"

General Gort tried to resist the grin that spread on his face. "Among other things," he said in a soft voice. "Their Majesties wish to be the first to congratulate two new members of the Royal Air Force. So, let's not keep them waiting, eh?"

Audrey was holding my hand. She squeezed it hard and smiled when I made eye contact. The room was silent, like we were in the eye of a hurricane, about to engulf the world in one of its biggest disasters. Barney's eyes flickered from his Victoria Cross to the general and then to me. I looked around the room at all the smiling, beaming, and glowing faces. An icy shiver sped down my spine. My dream had come true.

This was the beginning, although one thing was for sure. Starting this moment, this day, I would do my part as a pilot in the Royal Air Force.

I leaned over to Audrey and whispered in her ear, "Ever been to Buckingham Palace?"

BOOK 2 IN THE JOHN ARCHER SERIES:

BOMBS OVER BRITAIN

"A fascinating World War II evade and escape story." – Reviewer

Hunted by the Gestapo, John Archer faces his toughest mission yet.

As the newest pilot for the RAF in the heat of the Second World War, John Archer is determined to serve the Allies and defend London from the *Luftwaffe*. But as a young pilot with little experience, a face-off with a German fighter Ace could cost him his life.

When he's selected for a top-secret spy mission, Archer finds himself airdropped deep into Nazi-occupied Belgium on a death-defying quest to recover vital intelligence. Archer and his best friend and wingman Barney know that the Allied war effort could hinge on their success. Archer's only hope lies in flying out of Belgium–if he can escape the Luftwaffe, that is.

ALSO BY DANIEL WRINN

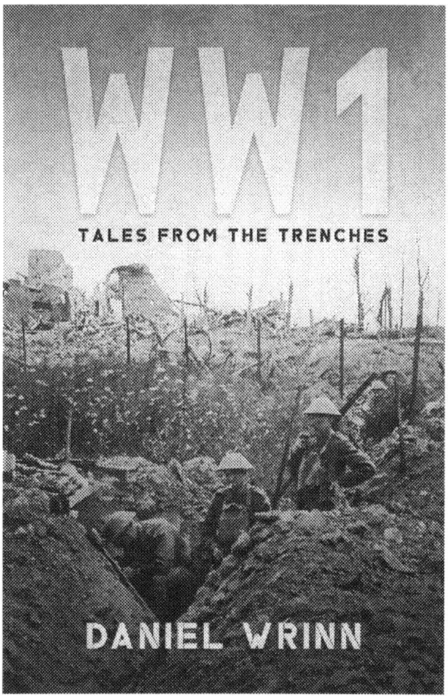

"Stunning stories that weave together the major fronts of WWI into a sweeping narrative." — Reviewer

The Great War left millions of civilians and soldiers maimed or dead.

Follow in the footsteps of the British, German, and American servicemen as they detail the life and struggles of war in a strange and foreign country. Uncover their mesmerizing, realistic stories of combat, courage, and distress in short stories told from the front lines.

Witness the creation of new technologies of destruction: tanks, planes, and submarines; machine guns and field artillery; poison gas and chemical warfare. It introduced U-boat packs and strategic bombing, unrestricted war on civilians and mistreatment of prisoners.

"A masterfully told story of triumph and redemption in a powerfully drawn survival epic." – Reviewer

Hero WWI Fighter Pilot Shot Down and Captured.

With an engaging and authentic retelling of his experiences as an escaped prisoner of war, this gripping account details the life and struggles of a captured pilot in 1917 war-torn Europe.

Lieutenant John Ryan couldn't wait to see action in WWI. He joined up with the British colors out of Canada. As one of several American pilots in the Royal Flying Corps before the US joined the war, he earned his wings and became an Ace through fierce air battles over the skies of Germany.

"A thrill a minute. You don't have to be a World War I buff to savor this one." — Reviewer

A daring captain. A ship full of weapons. And a sinister plot that could cripple Britain.

In the heart of world war one, a devious plan devised by the German navy led to Naval Officer Captain Karl Spindler embarking on a perilous and secret mission. His task—to deliver German weaponry to Ireland and spark what would become the Easter Uprising.

Departing from Norway with a disguised ship, Spindler undertook a perilous mission with a small crew and a hold full of explosives. If he succeeded, he could unleash a threat that would cripple the British war effort. But if he failed, a prisoner of war would be his fate…

Uncover a thrilling true story from the depths of world war one. Told with heart pounding detail that brings the lesser-known stories of the war to life, *Mission to Ireland* delivers a thrill a minute. You don't need to be a history buff to enjoy this one.

"Having served in Iraq, the comparisons to Wooten's World War I experiences with my own were remarkable." – Reviewer

Uncover a fascinating glimpse into WWI on the Mesopotamian front.

Few people truly know about Iraq's role in World War One. The stage of a desperate struggle against the Ottomans, the story of brave men who lived and served in this harsh landscape is often overshadowed by the battles in Europe and North Africa.

But now, this memoir explores the life and duty of Frank Wooten, an American, serving as a British officer in the Mesopotamian Motor Machine Gun Corps. Told with gripping detail and offering profound insights into the lesser-known Middle Eastern theater.

Recounting Frank's daily life on the front, his duties throughout the war, and the incredible people he met along the way, *Journey into Eden* is a fascinating book, perfect for anyone interested in the lesser-known stories of World War One, the history of the Iraq War, and the nature of life on the front.

ABOUT THE AUTHOR

Daniel Wrinn writes Military History & Action Adventure. A US Navy veteran and avid history buff, Daniel lives in the Utah Wasatch Mountains. He writes every day with a view of the snow capped peaks of Park City to keep him company. You can join his readers group and get notified of new releases, special offers, and free books here:

www.danielwrinn.com

Printed in Great Britain
by Amazon

17332541R00091